The Dudleys of Budleigh

The Dudleys of Budleigh

AN EAST DEVON COSY MYSTERY

P.A. NASH

First Published 2019
This edition 2021
www.eastdevoncosymysteries.com

DEDICATION

To the whole Nash family -
from Elsie's Bow, Shan, Franklyn to Resource Angel.
Love from PA.

ACKNOWLEDGEMENTS

Many of the places mentioned in this book do exist. Some of the places exist only in the figment of my imagination. I'll leave it to you to come to East Devon and Budleigh Salterton, in particular, to find out which are which.

"In the seventh hour of the night, on the seventh day of the year - you will die."

Anthony Buckerell received a note that simply delivered the fright of his complicated life.

Dudley's out to get me!" At 7.59, surrounded by police in a windowless locked cell, he did.

In the follow up to Cidered in Sidmouth, the genteel seaside resort of Budleigh Salterton is rocked by an impossible murder. Frank and Ella Raleigh find themselves reluctantly continuing as their delightful detective duo as delves into the lives of their suspects - each one named Dudley.

If you enjoy pacy whodunit cosy mysteries, then join Frank and Ella in the seaside resort of Budleigh Salterton getting to know some of the town's Dudleys as they head towards a traditional Golden Age denouement.

A gentle cosy read in the tradition of Midsomer and the two Agathas set in our glorious East Devon countryside.

Treasure the coastal walks. Uncover the clues. Solve the impossible mystery.

TABLE OF CONTENTS

CHAPTER 1
SEVENTEEN WORDS

Retirement is wonderful, Frank thought. No more pressure. No more stress. No more looking at the clock. No more living by other people's expectations. No more… well, everything.

It was a cold and frosty Tuesday morning in January. Christmas had come and gone, and last year's adventures had begun to fade into a hazy memory. Frank and Ella were strolling with Bella and George through the woods along the old railway track from the Bowd down towards Harpford.

They crossed the East Devon Way and followed the track down to Knapp's Lane, branched off to the right and ambled over the stone railway bridge into the village of Harpford past St Gregory the Great. At the Recreation Ground carpark, the couples bid each other farewell and Frank and Ella headed for Otterbury and home.

Parking the car on the gravel drive, Frank heard the phone ringing inside the house. He rushed indoors and picked it up just in time to hear the caller. "Thank heavens you're there, Elsie. Come quickly, I think Dudley's out to get me! He sent me a horrible warning…"

"Hello, this is 3511543?" said Frank.

There was a pause.

"Ah, you're not Elsie? That's not 3511534, is it?"

The phone went dead.

"3511534 ...3511534... 3511534," Frank repeated the number out loud whilst gesturing to Ella to find him a pencil or pen.

"I'm writing it down. You can relax. The last two digits were accidentally reversed. What was all that about?"

Frank sat down and explained to Ella. "A man said Dudley's out to get him. He thought he was phoning Elsie. He said that wasn't 3511534 and then put the phone down."

"Who's Elsie?"

"The only Elsie I know is WPC Knowle."

"I think you should try that number and see if it goes through to this Elsie. Explain to her what happened. Whilst you're doing that, I'll put the kettle on!"

Ella went into the kitchen. Before Frank called the number he found out and wrote down the number of the person who had called him. As the caller needed to urgently speak to Elsie, he saw no point in calling back. Frank dialled 3511534.

It rang for about ten seconds and Frank was about to cut off the call when a female voice said: "Hello, how can I help?"

"Hello," replied Frank. "Is that Elsie?"

"Yes, it is. I recognise that voice. It's Frank, isn't it? Frank Raleigh?"

"How did you know?"

"You're speaking to a policewoman. We're trained to remember things."

"Elsie, WPC Knowle," Frank interrupted.

"Yes, that's me. It's good to hear from you again. Is everything all right with Ella? She was such a brave lady."

"Yes, everything's great. I've just had a strange phone call. I think it was a wrong number. Someone said Dudley was out to get him and you had to come quickly."

"Ah, that's not the first time. I bet you've had a call from Anthony Buckerell. He's a solicitor over in Budleigh Salterton. He thinks someone is trying to kill him. He seems to me as somewhat of a lonely old soul. A bit pompous and self-righteous. For a solicitor, he gets very muddle-headed. He needs a friend, and he needs to get a life!"

Frank recognised the type. "A loner?"

"I guess he is, as far as his job will allow him to be."

"We used to have children like that at school. Always sat on their own in the corner of the playground. I used to have to work hard to make them feel part of a suitable social circle."

"Perhaps you could help here?"

"How?" Frank felt he was digging himself into a hole and he wasn't sure how to clamber out.

"Come with me and see him. Offer him a sympathetic ear and use your school-masterly listening skills."

"Hmm," Frank hesitated.

"I'll go over there later this afternoon. If you want, I'll pick you up from Otterbury and we'll listen to his story and see if we can both help."

Ella had come back into the room with a tray full of cups of tea and biscuits. She had heard the last part of Frank's part in the conversation. She nodded encouragingly.

"OK, it can't do any harm."

"Excellent, I'll pick you at about half three."

Frank said goodbye and put the phone down.

"Who was that?" Ella asked.

"WPC Knowle. I know she's called Elsie, but I can't bring myself to call her by her first name."

"It's her sign of authority."

"Yes, she'll always be WPC Knowle!" Frank went on to

recount the other half of the conversation to Ella.

"You'll be good for him. He sounds a bit paranoid. You'll soon sort him out!"

Frank sipped his tea and wondered what he'd let himself in for.

Budleigh Salterton has an undeserved reputation as God's waiting room. If you took the time to explore its many nooks and crannies, you would be delighted to find individualistic houses, picturesque back lanes, engaging architecture, a fascinating shopping area and a couple of old-fashioned tea shops gently competing for custom. The High Street appeared to be in a slight valley with all of its side roads leading uphill.

East of the town, the pebble beach had formed into a spit and was trying to strangle the mouth of the River Otter. Head westwards back towards the town and you walk below gentle sandstone cliffs before meeting a wide promenade backed by a variety of well-maintained seaside houses. Although it was now the middle of winter, there were still plenty of people walking along the level, spacious promenade, enjoying the salty sea air. The promenade, which hosted the South West Coast Path, waved the path on its way as it climbed westwards out of town and up towards the dizzy heights of West Down Beacon.

All along the mile-long seafront were seats and benches facing out across the pebble beach looking out at the wide expanse of Lyme Bay. Each summer, well-populated beach huts stood between the tarmac path and the beach. As the season ended, they were taken down and stored safely away from the ravages of any winter storms.

Budleigh Salterton was home to a plethora of clubs and societies. There were markets, walks and dramatic enterprises, sports clubs, even a flourishing Literature Festival. The town was too busy to be a Waiting Room.

Anthony worked in an office in the High Street above one of the flourishing gift shops that regularly blossom for a while in seaside towns.

WPC Knowle parked right outside the office and she pushed open a neat wooden door beside the shop front. They both climbed the stairs before WPC Knowle knocked on another door that had faded gold lettering announcing that they were entering the offices of Anthony Buckerell LLB, LLP.

No-one answered her knock, so she turned the door handle. The door was unlocked so they walked in.

A quiet, strained voice mumbled, "Come in."

"Too late, Anthony. We're already in!"

"Oh, it's you. Thank heavens!"

Anthony Buckerell was sat, or rather slumped, in a wooden varnished but padded Bankers Chair behind a large mahogany Executive desk. The desk was clear except for a pristine blotter, an old-fashioned telephone and a couple of leather-bound A4 books. The wording appeared to read "Law Society" on the front cover.

"Dudley wants to kill me!"

"Good afternoon, Anthony, may we sit down?"

"Yes, pull up a chair. I see you've brought a detective with you. Good afternoon, Chief Inspector, are you from Exeter?"

Frank sat down and smiled.

"Anthony, this is the gentleman you accidentally called earlier today. He's a sort of consultant. He's shadowing me and providing valuable feedback. You can rest assured that anything you say to either of us will be treated in a professional manner and in the strictest confidence.

"Good. I need all the help I can get!" Anthony was sweating and repeatedly ran his hand through his receding hair as if brushing it back out of his eyes.

"Where's Mrs. Aylesbeare?"

"She doesn't work today. She's part-time now. I don't want to speak about her. She's always nagging me."

WPC Knowle sat down and took out her notebook. "OK, Anthony, how may we help you?"

Anthony looked up at Frank before his eyes travelled around to WPC Knowle. Then he looked down at his desk. "Dudley's out to get me. He sent me a letter. It said that I would..."

He buried his face in one hand. With the other hand, he pushed a piece of paper across the desk.

Frank picked it up and read aloud the printed words:

"You will die in the seventh hour of the night on the seventh day of the year."

Frank turned the piece of paper over. Nothing else. Just those seventeen words.

WPC Knowle took out her phone and checked the date. "It's the sixth of January today. Tuesday, the sixth of January. That must mean tomorrow."

"I know! You needn't tell me what the date is. I know. Tomorrow. Tomorrow." His voice was becoming louder and more uncontrolled. "Tomorrow!" He shouted.

Frank put the note back on the table. "Who's Dudley?"

"I don't have any friends called Dudley. I don't really have people I can call friends."

"How do you know that Dudley is out to get you?"

"He sent me another note last week."

"Have you still got it?" Frank asked in a quiet but authoritative voice.

"Of course, I've still got it." The solicitor opened a drawer in the pedestal beside the desk and hauled out a batch of papers. He put them untidily on the desktop and then reached back into the drawer before extracting a single sheet of paper. He pushed that across the desk to Frank.

On an A4 size printed sheet Frank read "Dudley's gonna get you."

WPC Knowle was scribbling in her notebook. "That seems pretty clear. Dudley, whoever he or she is, wants to kill you tomorrow, Wednesday, sometime before eight o'clock in the evening."

Anthony looked up and, in a trembling,, bewildered voice croaked, "I don't want to die. I need your help. Keep me alive."

The policewomen finished writing in her notebook and smiled at the scared man.

"You shall get our help. First of all, you need to pack a bag. You are going away for a few days."

"Where?"

"Somewhere safe. Then you are going to stay with us all through tomorrow. We shall be with you for every minute of the day. No-one will get to you without having to get by us first."

WPC Knowle's confident tone brought some much-needed strength to the solicitor.

"I knew I was right to phone you. It's outrageous that some little nobody would make such threats to such an important man like myself."

Frank, for the first time, detected a reason why someone would want to kill this man.

"I suggest, Mr. Buckerell, that you do what the police-lady says. We'll go with you to your house. You then will pack a bag with clothes that will last you a couple of days."

"Is Mrs. Aylesbeare working here tomorrow?"

"Yes, I think so."

WPC Knowle snapped her notebook shut, stood up and faced the solicitor. "Get your coat. Leave a note for Mrs. Aylesbeare. Tell her you won't be in tomorrow and to cancel any appointments. Turn off the lights, lock up and set the alarm. We're taking you home."

Anthony Buckerell stood up and dutifully followed her list of commands. Frank picked up the two threatening pieces of paper and put them in an empty envelope he rescued from amongst the untidy pile of papers still scattered on the desk. WPC Knowle saw what he was doing and gave him a paper evidence bag. He slipped the letters into the bag and gave it back to WPC Knowle. "Fingerprints!"

The office was made secure. As Anthony locked the door, he ran his hand over the gold lettering. Like the rest of the office, it needed some attention. The three of them made their way downstairs to the police car.

WPC Knowle put the solicitor into the back seat of the police car and, having ascertained where he lived, drove off down the high street before turning off up past the church.

They soon arrived at the detached house on a very exclusive road in a very exclusive area of Budleigh Salterton. They went inside. WPC Knowle did a quick but thorough search of the house and then, finding it empty, instructed Anthony to sort out some belongings into a bag. Frank was, as usual, impressed by WPC Knowle's efficient manner. As they waited downstairs in the front room, he was compelled to ask her about her plans.

"Simple. We take him to a safe house tonight. Tomorrow we'll drive him around until the evening and then..." she faltered at this point in the plan.

"We need a place where nobody can reach him. Where he's safe and secure."

"Yes, we need to lock him away somewhere."

"Is Exeter jail available for the night?"

"No, but I was working the other day in the old unmanned Otterbury police station. It has a single cell in the middle of the building. There's no windows and one very secure steel door. There are surveillance cameras dotted all around. Nobody could get in or out without us knowing."

"Do the cameras work or are they dummies?"

"Actually, these ones do work!"

"Right. That seems like a good plan. Put PC Hydon on the front door and lock Mr. Buckerell in the cell."

"He's got to be safe there!"

CHAPTER 2
A RATHER POMPOUS MAN

Frank phoned Ella and she drove over from Otterbury to pick him up outside the Public Halls. On the journey home, Frank recounted the visit to Anthony Buckerell's office and house.

"They're putting him up somewhere in this area in, what they call, a safe house. Tomorrow WPC Knowle and PC Hydon are going to take him onto Dartmoor and keep moving around. Then, in the evening, we're going to guard him at Otterbury Police Station."

"Do you mean you and me?"

"No, WPC Knowle, PC Hydon and yours truly."

"How?"

"Well, Elsie didn't exactly tell me. I think the plans are on a need-to-know basis."

"Don't you need to know?"

"Not until tomorrow!"

Frank and Ella spent a quiet relaxing evening at home. Ella was certain that Anthony Buckerell was not sharing their restfulness. He'd be sitting there, wondering if this was to be his last night on earth. It was too horrific to contemplate so she turned on the TV and watched back-to-back episodes of Dad's Army.

Frank was sat in front of his computer screen researching Anthony Buckerell. He appeared to be single and well qualified. He had been working in Budleigh Salterton for eight years. He went to university at Oxford. He wasn't on any social media channels, but his name appeared on Facebook and Twitter quite regularly. Hardly any of the posts were complimentary. A few of them were downright rude. Both libel and slander laws appeared to be being broken in a few of the comments. Frank wondered whether Anthony Buckerell would be appealing to the full force of the law if he ever decided to peruse social media.

The main theme of the social media posts and the newspaper reports was that of a self-righteous, rather pompous man. That tallied with Frank's experience after their recent, brief meeting.

There was very little evidence that he had any real enemies. Now and again, a Dudley was mentioned in a newspaper report. No Dudleys were named in any Facebook or Twitter posts.

Despite the negative comments, he did appear to be good at his job. In fact, some may consider him to be too good. He stuck rigidly to the letter of the law. Researching through the local online newspaper, he did appear to win many of the cases with which he was involved. Frank assumed that this was the reason that he was able to charge what seemed like rather high fees. No wonder he lived in the affluent part of Budleigh Salterton.

Frank saved some of the most interesting links and articles into his Evernote account and then closed down the computer.

The next day time passed slowly as Frank and Ella waited for a phone call from Elsie. They didn't dare go out. A jigsaw on the dining room table saw remarkable progress made during the day. Eventually, in the late afternoon, it was Alf, PC Hydon, who phoned. He told Frank to meet them at the small local police station in Otterbury. Frank dressed up warmly in preparation for a cold, long night. Ella prepared sandwiches and snacks as well as a large flask of hot, sweet tea. She put a blanket and the refreshments into a small, branded sports bag - a relic of more active days.

Seeing as the station was in Otterbury, Frank was able to walk the ten minutes from their house. It was just after half-past five when he arrived. Alf, PC Hydon, was standing at the door. When he recognised Frank, he smiled. "Hello. Mind if I check the bag?"

He rooted around in the bag before taking out the refreshments and the blanket. He gave the blanket a good shake. "Looks like there's enough food and drink for the four of us!"

"You can thank Ella for that!"

"I will. In the morning."

Alf put everything back in the bag and moved aside. He opened the door and beckoned him in. "They're already in the cell. Just knock on the door."

The police station was normally unmanned. It had one cell which was surrounded by three linked rooms and a reception area. Although it was early evening, all the lights were on. Frank crossed the small reception area to a door on which were stencilled the words Holding Cell.

Frank knocked. WPC Knowle asked in a firm voice, "Who's there?"

Frank replied "Frank Raleigh. Your name is Elsie."

"Hold on, whilst I unlock the door."

The clang of keys sounded like the soundtrack of an ancient

horror movie. Eventually, the door opened.

"Come in and I'll lock the door behind you."

"Thanks." He had to push the door quite hard to make it move. It was heavy and felt extremely sturdy, extremely secure. Even if it were left unlocked, he didn't fancy his odds of rapidly exiting the room in an emergency.

WPC Knowle relocked the door and put the bunch of keys down underneath her chair. Frank looked around and placed the sports bag in the nearest corner - to the left of the door.

"Mind if I check the bag?"

WPC Knowle rooted around in the bag, taking out the refreshments and the blanket. She, like PC Hydon, gave the blanket a good shake. "Cor, you've got enough here to feed and fuel the four of us! Thanks."

"Ella's the one to thank!"

"I will. In the morning."

The cell, like the reception area, was brightly lit. There were three chairs and a fold-down bed. There was no window. The walls, like all the others in the building, appeared to be made of stone.

The three plastic chairs had been placed in a triangle with two of the chairs nearest the door. WPC Knowle sat in one of those two. Anthony, Mr. Buckerell, sat in the one furthest away from the door. Frank sat down in the one empty chair.

"I defy anyone to break in," he said. "Two steel doors, one locked, the other guarded by a man mountain. Stone walls all around us. It'd take a bomb to kill us!"

"Urgh!" groaned Mr. Buckerell. "Shut up!"

"Mr. Buckerell is not particularly enjoying today. He's eaten hardly anything, drank nothing and says he feels ill."

"So would you if....urgh," Mr. Buckerell groaned again.

"We called in at a doctor friend of mine near Princetown and he found him to be in the best of health."

"Do you trust this doctor?"

"With my life!"

"Are you sure?"

"Yes, the doctor is my dad!"

Frank's smile disguised his surprise.

"Even policewomen have fathers."

"Of course. So apart from that, has the day gone well?"

"It's been a breeze. We've driven around most of Dartmoor in an unmarked police car. Down some country lanes where the tarmac's been replaced by grass. We doubled back and forth all afternoon. No-one followed us. No-one knows we are here, except for my Sargent in Exeter and the Assistant Chief Constable. She's the one who gave me permission for all this skullduggery."

"How are you feeling, Mr. Buckerell?"

"Urgh!"

"He's not the most effusive of conversationalists," WPC Knowle smiled, "But then I'm not sure I would be in his situation."

Frank turned towards the silent solicitor. "Don't worry, Mr. Buckerell. We've put all this together to make certain you're safe. You'll be perfectly OK. This weekend, you'll be able to keep all your friends enthralled by this story. Next year, you'll probably be laughing about it!"

Mr. Buckerell just stared at Frank with a deep frown over his hooded, tired eyes. If looks could kill, Frank thought. Oops, perhaps, that wasn't the best phrase to use at the moment. He kept his ruminations to himself.

There was no clock in the cell. Every now and again, Frank surreptitiously looked at his watch. Quarter to seven. Time passed so slowly that it felt like midnight already. Frank poured three cups of tea. Two were drunk. The other turned cold.

At seven o'clock a distinct chill enveloped the cell. The seventh hour of the night. Nobody moved.

At ten past seven, WPC Knowle went to the door, took out her walkie talkie, and called out, "Everything OK, PC Hydon?"

There was a crackle of static before PC Hydon replied. "Yes, quiet as a graveyard out here."

"Urgh!" Mr. Buckerell was not amused.

"We'll check every ten minutes as planned. Unless the situation changes. Over and out."

At twenty past seven, WPC Knowle went to the door, took out her walkie talkie, and spoke into it, "Everything still OK, PC Hydon?"

"As quiet as a mouse."

"Speak to you in ten minutes."

She sat back down, took out her notebook and jotted down the events from seven o'clock.

At half-past seven, she again stood up and activated her walkie talkie. There was a crackle until she moved closer to the door. "Everything OK, PC Hydon?"

"Yep. It's getting boring out here."

"Good, that's exactly how we want it to be."

She sat back down. Mr. Buckerell was feeling the strain. His whole face was definitely paler than it was earlier.

"Are you OK, Mr. Buckerell?"

"Urgh! Course I am. When this is all over, you're taking me out to the nearest pub and buying me a slap-up meal!"

At twenty to eight, WPC Knowle again got up, went closer to the door and again activated the walkie talkie once more.

"Everything still OK, PC Hydon?"

"Yes, absolutely. Looks like it's been a fuss about nothing. No-one comes near the place. Even the dog walkers have given tonight a miss."

"Speak to you in ten minutes."

At ten to eight, a smile almost appeared on Mr. Buckerell's face. True, it may have been a grimace, but Frank gave him the benefit of the doubt that he was trying to smile.

Once more, WPC Knowle stood up, went to the door. Once more she activated the walkie talkie. "Everything OK, PC Hydon?"

There was silence. No crackle. No reply.

"PC Hydon, Alf, are you there?"

The strain was beginning to tell even with WPC Knowle.

For the third time, she asked: "PC Hydon, are you there?"

There was a crackle, then a small voice replied, "Sorry about that. Call of nature. When a man's got to go, then a man's got to go."

"Don't you ever do that again. Stay alert at all times. Speak to you in ten minutes."

Frank gazed at his watch as it moved slowly but surely towards the hour mark. At one minute to eight, Mr. Buckerell turned to him and started to say, "Eight? Urgh!".

"Seven fifty-nine," replied Frank.

Then the strangest thing happened. For the first time since Frank had entered the cell two and a half hours ago, Mr. Buckerell got up out of his chair. He glared convulsively around the room as if looking for someone. He staggered, almost drunkenly, towards the door, before clutching his heart. His whole body shook before with a terrifying groan he collapsed, hitting his head on the steel door and knocking over WPC Knowle, Frank and both their chairs in the process.

"Anthony?" cried WPC Knowle, "Anthony?"

She felt his wrist for a pulse. She felt again, this time frantically by his neck.

"Impossible. This is impossible," she exclaimed.

She activated her walkie talkie once more and shouted into it.

"Alf, call an ambulance. Now!!"

CHAPTER 3
A VERY BIZARRE SCENARIO

"The note said You will die in the seventh hour of the night on the seventh day of the year. And he did."

"But how? We were there by his side. The door was locked. No-one came in. No-one went past PC Hydon. We even had back-up. There were five undercover policemen stationed out of sight all around the building. Even PC Hydon didn't know they were there."

It was now ten o'clock. The last two hours had been hectic. WPC Knowles fumbled and stumbled but eventually opened the cell door. An ambulance had arrived within minutes from the local node point, according to the paramedics. Both Frank and Elsie knew it was useless.

"He was dead the moment he stood up. I could see that. It must have been a massive heart attack."

Frank nodded. "The strain and pressure were simply too much. Poor man. I didn't particularly like him, but no-one deserves to die like that."

Frank and WPC Knowle were sat in the reception area of the small police station still shocked and stunned.

"A minute later and the note would have been completely wrong."

Frank had a puzzled expression on his face. "Do you suppose

someone, somehow knew about his heart?"

"Even if they did, how did they know he would fall down dead at that precise moment?"

"You're right. It's impossible."

"Who was his doctor?"

"No idea at the moment. I presume it's someone in Budleigh. We'll need to find out and contact them."

PC Hydon opened the outside door and Ella pushed past him. She immediately went up to Frank. He stood up and they hugged each other as if scared to ever let go.

Frank had phoned Ella as soon as the Scene of Crime team and the detectives had finished their initial examination of the site.

PC Hydon went into one of the other rooms and returned with two more chairs. Ella had brought a huge flask with her. She quickly poured out four cups of very hot, very sweet tea.

They all sat down facing each other, Ella with one arm draped over Frank's shoulders.

"Nobody came by me. Even when I had my call of nature, I was only metres away. I could see the door. No-one went in. No-one came out. Honestly!" PC Hydon was quite shaken.

"And even if they did, the door was locked. I saw Elsie, WPC Knowle, lock the door and then later struggle to unlock it."

"But no-one came past me."

"I believe you, Alf," said Frank.

"It's impossible."

Ella took her arm off Frank and turned to the others. "I have no idea what went on this evening. Why don't you all tell me the story from beginning to end? It might help. You may be able to work out how it all happened."

"Wait a minute," said WPC Knowle. "Why are we worrying? Mr. Anthony Buckerell died of a heart attack. Frank and I both saw it happen before our very eyes. No-one killed him. There is no murder to investigate. Only a tragic accident."

"I seem to remember you said that exact phrase last time!" Ella responded.

"Fair play. But this time, Frank and I both saw what happened."

"WPC Knowle is correct. We both saw the strain and stress he was under. He started to go pale about ten minutes or so before he died."

"It just seems a very bizarre scenario," Ella mused.

"Yes," said WPC Knowle. "Were we right to look after him so carefully? Should we have brought him here? Is it our fault he's dead?"

She voiced exactly what Frank had been thinking.

WPC Knowle's phone rang. She answered it and quickly moved off into one of the side rooms to talk to whoever was calling her.

The other three could hear little of the conversation except for Elsie's regular comment of "Yes sir."

When she came back into the room she looked pale and even more shocked.

"What's the matter?" Ella asked.

"That was the Assistant Chief Constable. They're rushing through the postmortem. If he did die from a heart attack, then I'm in for a disciplinary review. It could mean dismissal."

"That's ridiculous," Ella cried.

"No," replied Elsie, "that's the way the ACC likes to work. Give them enough rope to hang themselves. If it goes wrong, it's not her fault."

PC Hydon stood up. "Well, I'm off duty now. So are you, WPC Knowle. I suggest we all go home, get a good night's sleep and see what the morning brings."

Frank stood up as well. "An excellent suggestion."

"Elsie, we're on the other end of the phone. We'll do whatever we can to help." Ella gripped Elsie's arm and smiled.

"Thanks. Both of you. I'll let you know when I know anything more. Goodnight."

The four of them left the Scene of Crime team to their jobs and exited the building.

The morning was dismal. Persistent rain and a biting cold wind. It was symptomatic of both Frank and Ella's mood as they stared out of the lounge window. They couldn't see Mutter's Moor. It was covered in low cloud.

Just before lunchtime, the phone rang.

"How would you like to be unpaid consultants in a murder investigation?"

"Is that you, Elsie, I mean WPC Knowle?" Frank had picked up the phone and was surprised by the confident, enthusiastic voice on the other end.

"Yes. I'm told the postmortem showed up some pretty amazing facts."

"Tell us more!"

"I can't - I haven't read it yet! The four of us are going to meet at Anthony's house in about half an hour. OK?"

"Yes, of course. See you there."

Frank and Ella arrived at Anthony Buckerell's house exactly twenty-eight minutes later. In the gravel drive were two police cars, one needing a clean and the other looking spotlessly immaculate. The rain had stopped but the cold wind still prevailed. They got out and made their way to the front door. The door was guarded by a police constable who must have been half the size of Alf Hydon. He opened the door and stepped aside to let the pair in.

"In here," WPC Knowle called from the front room.

Standing in the middle of the room was a police lady who looked and acted as if she were of vastly superior rank.

"So, this is Frank and Ella Raleigh?"

"Good afternoon. I expect you're the Assistant Chief Constable," said Frank.

"Yes, absolutely. How did you know?"

"I recognised your rank badge."

"Excellent. Please sit down. Don't worry. We've already had the room checked for evidence."

Frank and Ella sat together on a plush sofa. The ACC took one of the armchairs and WPC Knowle sat in another whilst PC Hydon sat on a wooden chair near the window.

"Community relationships are so important," the ACC began. "I've heard the story about you in Sidmouth. I'd like you to help out WPC Knowle and PC Hydon with our little problem here in Budleigh Salterton."

Ella gripped Frank's hand.

"I'm not sure my wife is quite ready to step back into her crime-fighting role."

"Is that true, Mrs. Raleigh? Because if you'd rather not help us, then I perfectly understand."

Ella sat there silently contemplating. Eventually, she said, "I'd like to know more before I answer."

"Fair enough. Let me tell you, if there is any hint of any verbal or physical violence directed towards you, my officers will whisk you away from the situation and that will be the end of your contribution. I will NOT endanger any member of the public at any time in any of our investigations."

"Fine words," mumbled Frank.

"Not just fine words but true words. I mean what I say."

"I think I believe you," began Ella.

"However, if my police colleagues decide to let you in on any evidence that comes their way, you are to treat it as confidential. Short of signing the Official Secrets Act, you are NOT to share our way of working with other members of the general public."

"We understand." Frank nodded.

"Yes, but why you are telling us all this official mumbo-jumbo?" added Ella. "I thought the solicitor, Mr. Buckerell, died from a heart attack?"

"So did we. But it seems my colleague's first impressions were somewhat off the mark. Anyway, I need to go to an important meeting in Exeter and as much as I'd love to stay here and help, I'm going to leave you in the very capable hands of WPC Knowle and her colleague, PC Hydon. I have given PC Hydon the findings of the initial postmortem."

The ACC got up. "Oh, and one other thing. If you should decide to help us as community consultants, then on behalf of the Devon and Cornwall Constabulary, thank you!"

And with that, she left the room, shouted: "I'm ready, George." There was the sound of heavy boots from somewhere within the house. Thirty seconds later the immaculately spotless police car burst into life and the ACC had left the premises.

After the ACC had left, the four of them sat down waiting to hear about the postmortem.

Ella asked the most obvious opening question, "What does the postmortem say?"

PC Hydon read from a piece of paper. "It's only the preliminary findings but they say he definitely died from a heart attack.

"Well, that's what we saw," Frank added.

"But," continued Alf, "the heart attack was caused by a reaction to some as yet unknown chemical."

"Is that murder?" Ella exclaimed, "But how?"

"It says here that they found a series of puncture marks in his arm. Some of them are very recent - maybe the last couple of days. They think the chemical could have been injected."

"Could they be self-administered?"

"We don't know. Yet."

"Could he have swallowed something?"

"That's impossible."

"Exactly," said Elsie. We were with him for the whole day. He hardly ate any food. He drank very little liquid. My dad and I were the only people who had any contact with him yesterday. My dad is a doctor, not a murderer and I certainly didn't kill him."

"Anything else?"

"No, nothing that we didn't know already. He died instantly."

"Does that mean that the chemical killed him instantly? If so, it happened inside a locked police station cell with no windows with two highly respectable witnesses in attendance. There was also one way into the building, and it was guarded by the police force's largest officer."

"It must have happened last night at the police station. Did he get an opportunity to inject himself?"

"No, Frank and I were sitting in the room beside him. We didn't take our eyes off him for nearly two and a half hours. And nobody got past PC Hydon."

"Perhaps there were chemicals already in the room," said Frank.

"I don't see how but we'll need to get that checked."

"Or it was put on his clothes and he rubbed against it."

"We'll test them."

"Perhaps someone fired a blowpipe dart at him."

"Into a room with no window?"

"Or a drone dropped poison on him."

They all looked at each other. Ella burst out laughing. "I think we're getting into the realms of fantasy. Let's look at this logically."

There was a short period of silence as each of them gathered their thoughts together.

Ella started the brainstorming session herself. "We need to find this doctor. Find out if they injected him with anything. Search this house to see if any syringes or needles are lying around...."

"We already searched," interrupted Alf.

"Yes, but did you know what you were searching for?"

"No, we searched thoroughly," said PC Hydon in a gruff very official voice. "We looked for medicine bottles, tablets and chemicals. So far we've found nothing of that kind of thing here."

"We have, however, found the name of his doctor," added Elsie. "It's a Doctor D. Moore."

Frank smiled. "Dudley?"

"Wouldn't that be a coincidence?"

Ella was on a roll again. "Talking of Dudley, shouldn't we go through his case files and find out if any Dudleys have a grievance against him?"

"Good idea. If we speak to Mrs. Aylesbeare, his office secretary, surely she'll know?"

"Then, if we find any Dudleys, we need to interview them and see if we can discover a motive."

"Motive. Means. Opportunity. Alibi." Alf's voice listed the mantra.

"I'll need to get the whiteboard out of the garage once again at this rate!"

Elsie had been jotting the bullet points down in her notebook. "Right, here's a plan of campaign. One - we interview the Doctor. Two - we meet up with Mrs. Aylesbeare. Three - we conduct a thorough search of the house and his office - now we know what we're looking for!"

Alf was not amused.

"Seeing as you've been to his office before," said Ella to Elsie, "why don't you and Frank go there?"

"Alf and I will search this place once more. I bet there are outbuildings and probably a loft and a cellar."

"There is," said Alf, "and they were very messy."

"Well, I'm going to drive home and change into some old clothes. I'll be back in an hour." She got up and left the room before anyone else could agree or disagree.

Alf got up as well. "I'd better change into my search togs. I'll get Ella a couple of pairs of official disposable gloves and footwear."

Elsie turned to Frank. "Let me phone Mrs. Aylesbeare and get her to meet us at the office. I found her number in poor old Mr. Buckerell's telephone book. He had a really old-fashioned book by the phone in the hall."

Frank wandered around the house whilst Elsie phoned Mrs. Aylesbeare. It was a typical 1930s detached house. The sort of house that would play its part in a Miss Marple murder novel in a quaint Devon village.

The house was tidy, no dust on the wooden polished floorboards or around the light fittings and appeared to be in good condition. For a bachelor, he was either an exceedingly good housekeeper or he employed one.

"Frank?"

WPC Knowle had finished her phone call.

"Mrs. Aylesbeare will meet us at his office in twenty minutes. She seems very keen to help us."

"Good," said Frank. "Let's walk there. Walking is good for your wellbeing."

"Yes, I know, it gets the brain cells churning."

"Exactly. I'm looking forward to meeting Mr. D. Moore, the Doctor. If he's not our man, then we'll just have to widen our search. I reckon our murderer is one of the Dudleys of Budleigh."

CHAPTER 4
CHECK THE COMPLAINTS

Frank and WPC Knowle arrived at the office of the late Anthony Buckerell at the same moment as Mrs. Aylesbeare. They followed her up the stairs in single file. Mrs. Aylesbeare unlocked the office door and welcomed them in.

"Please enter, my dears. Isn't this exciting?" She was a small well-rounded lady, wearing an ankle-length patterned woollen coat and a flowery yellow hat. She carried a large brown corduroy handbag. She reminded Frank, at once, of how he imagined Miss Marple would look straight from the pages of one of Agatha Christie's novels.

"This is Frank Raleigh, he's a consultant appointed by the Assistant Chief Constable to provide a community-based viewpoint and I'm WPC Knowle. We spoke on the phone a little while ago."

"Yes, I know." She smiled in a welcoming manner. "Please sit down, make yourself comfortable and ask me anything you like."

WPC Knowle began by explaining why they were here in the office. "We thought, at first, that Mr. Buckerell had died from a heart attack. However, our pathology people think that Mr. Buckerell may have been poisoned."

"Poisoned. How astonishing!" Instead of showing some form

of emotional distress or shock, Mrs. Aylesbeare appeared animated and even delighted.

"So we're investigating to see if anyone had a reason to kill him."

"He didn't die by having poison in his coffee, did he? I mean, that would be the perfect crime for Mr. Buckerell. He loved his coffee. Every morning he took his table by the window at Earls. Oh, my word. Poisoning by coffee would be perfect. He didn't, did he?"

"Not as far as we know."

"Good. However, he wouldn't have been the first."

"Pardon?"

"The Queen of Crime. Black Coffee. She wrote that as a play in 1930." She paused to take a breath. She had the perfect Miss Marple voice.

WPC Knowle took the opportunity to get in a word edgeways. "How do you know all this?"

"The little grey cells, my dear!"

"Interesting," said Frank.

"The truth is never horrible, only interesting."

"I don't understand you?"

"Dame Agatha wrote that in Black Coffee. Surely, you've heard of Dame Agatha Christie. The world's greatest detective authoress. I would say, perhaps, even the world's greatest authoress, full stop."

"Lots would agree with you," ventured Frank, "but..."

"And she was Devon born and bred!"

"Yes. Lovely." WPC Knowle thought she had lost total control of the situation." Let's get back to the matter in hand!"

"Sorry, my fault," Frank apologised.

"We need your help."

Another expectant smile appeared on the old lady's face. "Fire away. This is so exciting, my dears!"

"We think that somehow Mr. Buckerell may have had some problems with a Dudley. Do you recall any Dudleys in any of his cases in the past few years?"

"I'd have to have a think and then go through the files. We kept quite meticulous records, you know."

"I'm sure."

Frank jumped in again. A sparkler this time rather than dynamite. "Was Doctor Dudley Moore ever a client?"

"Who? I don't know a doctor named Dudley Moore. He was a jazz pianist, wasn't he? Mr. Buckerell used to love him and those two other British pianists - Roy Budd and George Shearing. Yes, he loved the jazz piano. Then there were the Americans like Erroll Garner, Fats Waller and dear old Oscar Peterson. We used to have the music on sometimes in the office. Some of it, I liked but I used to really love the more romantic pianists. Richard Clayderman. Russ Conway. Liberace."

"A Doctor called Dudley Moore, not a pianist?"

"I was just coming to that. If you'd meant Daniel Moore, that would be another matter. Daniel Moore is, or should I say, was, Mr. Buckerell's doctor. He used to visit him every month for his vitamins."

"Doctor Moore used to visit him?"

"No, Mr. Buckerell used to visit Dr Moore. Mostly in his surgery. Occasionally, if Mr. Buckerell forgot the appointment, then Dr Moore might come here."

"For vitamins?"

"Yes, get me more. He used to say. I think he said it as a joke. One of his very rare jokes! Mr. Buckerell wasn't much for jokes. "

Ella arrived back at Mr. Buckerell's house to find PC Hydon standing at the front door holding her protective clothing. A pair of what looked like white plastic bags for her feet and similar-looking gloves for her hands. She laughed as she put them on. "I feel very much like a professional policewoman now I'm wearing these. Do I need a bodysuit as well?"

"No, I don't think that will be necessary."

Ella wasn't quite sure if PC Hydon was joking or being serious. She decided that discretion was the better part of valour. She stood there and awaited further instructions.

"Right. We're going to be looking for syringes, needles or any form of suspicious tablets, bottles or chemicals."

"OK, where do we start?"

"In the rubbish bins. We went through them but as you said earlier, I expect we didn't search very thoroughly!"

"I didn't mean…"

"Well, I'll check the upstairs rooms and you check out the rubbish bins. As you probably know, there's three types of bins, general rubbish, recyclables and food. Best, if you check all three!"

He went through the house to the back door and led Ella out to the back of the garage. The bins were spaced out against the garage wall. In front of each bin was a large square of black plastic. PC Hydon lifted up each bin in turn and deposited the contents onto the corresponding black plastic.

"Enjoy," he said as he walked back towards the house.

Ella spent the next hour up to her elbows in the rubbish. There wasn't too much general rubbish, but it took Ella a while to sort meticulously through it. She made certain that no needle had been hidden in any piece of rubbish. She picked out one pill bottle and put it to one side.

The recyclable rubbish was treated in the same way. There was far more of it. She went through newspapers, empty envelopes and cardboard packaging. There was no sign of any incriminating material apart from one half of a plastic medicine spoon. She spent a long time unsuccessfully searching for the other half.

The food bin was more challenging and infinitely messier. The thin plastic bags Mr. Buckerell had used to contain the food waste had split open. The smell of rotten vegetables and mouldy bread coupled with a mountain of discarded tea bags reminded Ella of bygone days dealing with sick children. Days she thought she'd never have to go through again!

There was what looked like unfinished cauliflower cheese, a mound of potato peelings and what might have been the remains of a takeaway curry. Ella carefully and cautiously went through the food waste feeling for any needles or discarded tablets. After a fruitless 20 minutes, she was convinced that Mr. Buckerell or any other unknown person did not dispose of any incriminating material in any of the three rubbish bins.

She called out to PC Hydon. "I'm finished down here."

A bathroom window opened, and PC Hydon stuck his head out and looking down shouted, "Did you find anything I might have missed?"

"Only a.."

"Don't tell me. You found a pill bottle and half a plastic medicine spoon?"

"How did you know?"

"I found them when I searched through it all."

"I'm sorry I doubted you."

"That's OK. The dustmen are coming tomorrow so you'll have to return it all into the correct bins. Good luck!"

PC Hydon's head disappeared, and the bathroom window was closed.

Back at the solicitor's office, Mrs. Aylesbeare was having more luck than Ella.

She had a pile of well-filled folders on her desk. "I've found fourteen Dudleys. Some of them are very superficially involved whilst others are essential parts of a case."

WPC Knowle and Frank drew up a chair each and sat down on either side of Mrs. Aylesbeare's desk. She handed over one file at a time giving a brief word of guidance or information as she did so.

The next hour was spent in complete silence save for a few comments such as "Well, I never." Or "Very interesting." Both Frank and WPC Knowle took copious notes.

When the final file was handed back to Mrs. Aylesbeare, they looked at each other and smiled. "What did you make of that, Frank?"

"Some very interesting cases but one thing stood out for me above everything else."

"Let me guess? Hold on for a moment, whilst I write your next comments down!"

"Oh, a mind-reader as well as a police officer!" Mrs. Aylesbeare clapped her hands in delight. "Go on, Mr. Raleigh."

Frank took centre stage and addressed the expectant audience!

"Four of these Dudleys..." He paused for effect. "...made complaints of one sort or another!"

"Exactly what I've written down here in my notebook." WPC Knowle held it up for Frank to see. The words "CHECK THE COMPLAINTS" were written in capital letters!

Mrs. Aylesbeare chuckled and clapped her hands once more in delight. "Progress!"

"Right, I think, as a starting point we must concentrate on

these four."

"Let's gather the four files together," said WPC Knowle. "I wrote down Dudley Gosford-Feniton."

Mrs. Aylesbeare quickly flipped through the files before passing the correct one to WPC Knowle.

"Dudley Weston!" Again Mrs. Aylesbeare responded.

"Dudley Musbury." And again.

"And last, but not least, Dudley Widworthy."

WPC Knowle gathered the four files together and placed them neatly on the desk. "Put the others away so we don't muddle anything up."

"Now Mrs. Aylesbeare, are you able to tell us anything about these four characters?"

"Absolutely!" She leaned forward as if to impart some newly discovered secret. "Mr. Gosford-Feniton claimed that Mr. Buckerell swindled him out of an inheritance. I think it was something to do with a forged birth certificate. He'd regularly write to us about some bogus complaint or another. The letters arrived, like clockwork, on March 18th every year. Almost like it was an anniversary or some special date. There was never any specific complaint just vague innuendos!"

"Dudley Weston?"

"Oh, he was silly. He claimed that Mr. Buckerell was up to all sort of things. Again Mr. Buckerell just dismissed it. He called it pathetic."

"Dudley Musbury was a sad case. His wife was seriously injured in a car accident. It quite turned Mr. Musbury's mind. They had almost been friends up till then."

"Almost?" queried Frank.

"Well, to be honest, Mr. Buckerell didn't have any friends."

"And Dudley Widworthy?"

"He had a business selling herbal medicines. It went

bankrupt. Blamed Mr. Buckerell for some reason. But Mr. Widworthy was a terrible businessman. He had no idea."

"So, we have a connection." WPC Knowle was still furiously writing away in her notebook. "Four Dudleys each with a grievance of some sort. They each live in or around Budleigh."

Frank's face broke into a grin. "The Dudleys of Budleigh."

Back at Mr. Buckerell's house, Ella and PC Hydon continued their search.

"Has he got a safe?"

"Yes, a really old rusty thing in the corner of his study. It was very small. I picked it up and gave it a shake. There was nothing in there."

Ella could imagine the scene. "Show me where it is."

She followed PC Hydon into the study and sure enough, in the corner, stood a medium-sized safe.

"You picked that one and shook it?"

"Yes, it's quite light!"

He stooped and, with a straight back, gently lifted the safe up. He gave it a shake before placing back down on the ground. He wasn't even out of breath.

"How did you know it was empty?"

"I couldn't hear anything rattling around. Could you?"

"Do loose pieces of paper rattle around?"

"No, but… Oh, I see. What a fool I am. No wonder I'm not a detective yet."

Ella looked at the safe. There was a keypad with letters of the alphabet on it. "Hmm, either we need a dictionary or a huge stroke of luck."

"I don't believe in luck. Just hard work."

"Now, if you were Mr. Buckerell, what would you use as a password to get into this safe?"

For the next twenty minutes, they tried all sorts of words and letter combinations. They looked around the room at titles of books. Months of the year. Kings and Queens of England. Famous and infamous names. Nothing opened the safe door.

"Anthony?"

"No!"

"Wait a minute. We should have tried this one first of all."

"What one?"

"Dudley!"

CHAPTER 5
THE VERBAL ABOUT HERBAL

The safe door swung open with quiet ease.

"What's inside?" asked Ella expectantly.

PC Hydon pulled out a sheaf of paper. He took a look at the top piece and then shuffled through the remainder.

"Well, I never. Looks like letters. They're all letters. No envelopes, just letters."

He turned back to the topmost letter and began reading it silently to himself.

"How could I have missed these? I just assumed." He tutted and pointed a finger at himself. "Never assume, Alf, never assume!"

"What does it say?" Ella was getting more than a little exasperated. She was normally a patient person.

"It's a letter of complaint from a Dudley Widworthy."

"He's our poisoner, then!" Ella jumped and made as if to leave the room.

"Where are you going?"

"To telephone Frank and WPC Knowle."

"No. Wait. There's more."

"What do you mean?"

"The next letter is from Dudley."

"Dudley as well?"

"No, Dudley Musbury. It's a letter of complaint."

"Check the next one."

"Another Dudley. This one's from Dudley Gosford-Feniton."

"Another one?"

"Yes, except this one is also from Dudley Gosford-Feniton. And this one. And this one. And another."

PC Hydon continued leafing through the papers. "Ten of them. All from Dudley Gosford-Feniton."

"Fascinating! Our Mr. Buckerell was not a popular person with Dudleys!"

"Yes, here's another Dudley. This one's called Dudley Weston."

"Any more?"

"No, that's the last one. Four Dudleys."

"Four suspected poisoners!"

"I'm bagging these up before we wipe any more evidence off them."

PC Hydon soon had the letters safely stored away. "Why didn't I check the safe properly?"

"Can't be helped. At least, we've got some form of a motive."

"You mean that one of these Dudleys was so annoyed with Mr. Buckerell that they went beyond writing letters and took it further?"

"Exactly!"

"Now we can contact WPC Knowle and Frank."

There was a thump, thump, thump of boots up the stairs. The office door flew open, and an angry middle-aged man crashed into the room.

"Where is he? Where is that snide little weasel? I've reached the end of my tether. He's going to pay for this."

"Good afternoon, sir. I'm WPC Knowle. How can I help you?"

"I don't care who you say you are. Where is he? He won't answer my messages. This time, I've had..." The man blundered to a halt, like an oil tanker whose brakes take a while to have the desired effect.

"WPC Knowle. A police constable. That's why I'm wearing my police uniform. Good afternoon!"

"Good afternoon, er, ma'am."

"That's better. Frank, could you just knock on the office door for me?"

Frank went to the door and gently tapped on it.

WPC Knowle called out in a pleasant, welcoming voice: "Come in. Hello, how may we help you?"

The angry man had found the diversion beneficial. He had calmed down. He saw Mrs. Aylesbeare sitting at her desk.

"Good afternoon."

Mrs. Aylesbeare, barely suppressing a grin of glee, asked, "How may I help you, my dear?"

"I'd like to speak to that... to Mr. Buckerell. Is he here? Is he hiding from me?"

"I'm afraid that you won't be able to speak to Mr. Buckerell today, sir."

"What about tomorrow?"

"No, sir, not tomorrow, nor the day after, nor..." Mrs. Aylesbeare couldn't keep up the act any longer. "Sir, he's dead."

"Dead?"

The once angry man stood there immobilised, unable to know what to do next.

"Sit down, please, Mr....?"

"Widworthy. Dudley Widworthy."

PC Hydon carefully and slowly locked up the house, determined not to commit any further breach of police protocol. Ella waited in her car. Eventually, he completed all of his meticulous tasks and climbed sturdily into the passenger seat clutching his bag of evidence.

"Right. I decided to just go over to Mr. Buckerell's office with this. We can all discuss it there. There's no need to phone. We'll be at his office in ten minutes."

Ella turned to him. "If you're sure?"

"Drive on, please."

"How can he be dead? I saw him only a couple of days ago. I wrote him a letter just last week. He never replied. I got fed up with waiting and… he's dead?"

"What was the letter about?"

"I was complaining about his handling of my business. He took me for a mug!"

"Perhaps you'd better tell us the whole story. Begin at the beginning and all that," said Frank soothingly.

"Yes, it'll be good to get it off my chest. Someone around here needs to know the full facts."

"Do you mind if I take notes?" WPC Knowle already had her notebook and pen in hand.

"No." Dudley Widworthy looked around as if expecting to see Anthony Buckerell appear from one of the dark corners of the room.

"It started about eight years ago. I met Mr. Buckerell at a Budleigh Chamber of Trade meeting. We got talking about the

NHS and how their medicines didn't seem to work. He was a great believer in vitamins. Somehow,, we got onto herbal medicines. Self-medicating, he called it. I asked him where he would get such medicines from and he said there was nowhere around here. Instantly, a light went on in my head."

"Why?"

"Well, I'd been looking for a new business idea. My previous business had just been jogging along. I was an importer of exotic plants but there wasn't much profit in it. I went home and did some research and saw the potential as a supplier of herbal medicine here in Budleigh Salterton. The place is full of old biddies with illnesses. They call Budleigh Salterton 'God's waiting room'. I thought if I could tap into the market, there may be lots of money to be made."

"I came to you in good faith, Anthony. I thought you were my friend as well as my solicitor."

Well, Dudley, you are your own worst enemy sometimes. Let's look at your business decisions over the past two years, shall we?"

"Not another one of your lectures?"

"Sometimes, Dudley, the best way forward is to look back and learn from one's mistakes. Your first mistake was to buy too much stock at the very beginning without identifying who you were going to sell it to. Secondly, linked to that, you paid far too high a price for it. If you're buying that much, you could have demanded a huge discount. Or, at least, negotiated, some of the stock as sale or return."

"It was all from South America. They're difficult to deal with."

"Then there was Mrs. Westdown. Of all the people to suffer a reaction from one of your herbal tablets, she would not have been my first choice. She's a regular gossip of the highest order. Your name was mud, as soon as she entered that nursing home."

"Typical of my bad luck."

"Did you research the side effects? Did you check she was not allergic to any of the ingredients? No, you did not. Then your next mistake was to move into bigger premises. You could hardly pay your business rates or the shop rental for that place in Rolle Road. Why would you want to move into that monstrosity in the High Street?"

"Kerb appeal. Bigger footfall."

"No, vanity, pure vanity. I warned you against it. You didn't listen, did you?"

"I did listen. It was the way you warned me. You were so arrogant, so high and mighty, that I vowed to prove you wrong."

"You didn't, did you? No, the most recent mistake was not entirely your fault. No one thought that internet shopping would take hold so quickly. Still, then, you could have seen the opportunity. You didn't even have a website. You could have sold so much of your overpriced stock online."

"And now, I'm broke. Bankrupt. I blame you. You make me want to kill you!"

"Now threats like that could get you into even more trouble!"

"You should have stopped me. Given me better advice."

"Would you have listened?"

"I would have listened if you'd advised me in the right way."

"Well, I'm advising you now. Sell your stock, close down the shop and cut your losses."

"What choice do I have?"

"None at all."

"But who's going to buy my stock?"

"How much do you need to pay off your creditors and close

down the shop lease?"

"You know how much. You did all the calculations on that napkin there whilst we were drinking our coffees."

"Well, that's my offer. I've circled it to make sure you understand the exact amount."

"What! You are a nasty, vicious swindler. That'll leave me with nothing. No job, no assets, no prospects."

"That's the way it is in business. Sometimes you win, sometimes you lose."

"And I've lost big time!"

"I'll sort out an agreement for the stock. I'll call around with it tomorrow. I must be going. I'll leave you to pick up the bill. Call it my fee for all this free advice!"

"He bought me out" Dudley Widworthy concluded. "All my stock was gone - just like that. I found out a short while later that he'd sold the lot to an internet start-up company based in Exeter for a colossal profit. The internet company went bust a couple of years later, but he didn't care. He'd made his profit out of me."

Frank nodded in sympathy. There was enough resentment and desire for revenge in Dudley Widworthy's eyes. Were those the eyes of a murderer? WPC Knowle was still furiously writing notes in her black notebook.

Mrs. Aylesbeare was not impressed at all. "It was all your own fault, Mr. Widworthy. You shouldn't have taken so many risks. Now you're blaming poor Mr. Buckerell. All your verbals. And he can't answer you back, my dear. All your verbal about herbal!"

Frank wondered how long she'd been storing up that comment!

Dudley Widworthy's anger was returning. "I don't think it's

any of your business. You're just a secretary. What's more, you're his secretary!"

WPC Knowle had stopped writing. "Mr. Widworthy, calm down. There was no need for that."

"Sorry," he grumpily replied without looking at Mrs. Aylesbeare.

"We'd like to ask you a few questions, seeing as you are here. Just informal questions. I won't even caution you!"

"Most obliged, I'm sure."

WPC Knowle ignored the sarcasm. "I'm interested in these exotic plants of yours. Are any of them poisonous?"

"Some can be, I suppose. If you used their leaves in the wrong way."

"How?"

"Well, you could ground the leaves down into a powder."

Frank was intrigued. "Did you ever do that?"

"I read a few books about it, but it was too much hassle. You had to mix the powder with some other powders. I didn't have all of the plants. It was like being back in chemistry class at school. The amounts have to be so exact to have the maximum impact. And who was I going to use it on? I could have killed someone!"

"Someone like Anthony Buckerell?"

"No, look here! You said he was dead." He paused. His brain was whirring. "How did he die?"

"We think he may have been poisoned."

"Oh, I see your game. Plants, powders, poison. Blame it on Dudley. Everybody else does. I'm not standing for that." He stood up, clumsily knocking the chair over in his haste.

"You can't prove anything. You'd have arrested me if..."

"Mr. Widworthy, calm down. No-one's accusing you of..."

"Pull the other one!" He moved towards the office door. Frank stood up as if to stop him from leaving. “Get out of my way, unless you want some knuckles on your chin. I used to box when I was younger.”

He reached the door, opened it and stormed out, slamming the door behind him. The sound reverberated around the room. There was a crashing commotion on the stairs that lasted for over half a minute. WPC Knowle put away her notebook and was just about to stride across the room to investigate when the door opened once more.

CHAPTER 6
DEATH IS NOTHING AT ALL

In came Mr. Widworthy with a dejected and forlorn expression on his face. "I'd like to apologise for my behaviour."

"That's better, sir," said PC Hydon as he entered the room.

"Of course, I'd be happy to assist the police in any possible way."

"We may need to speak to you again. Just give your name, contact address and phone number to PC Hydon. He'll see you safely off the premises."

After Dudley Widworthy had quietly left, Ella made sure he had closed the door before she shared the discoveries with Frank and WPC Knowle.

"We found some papers in the safe. They were all letters of complaint. There were four Dudleys amongst them."

"Let me guess. Dudley Widworthy?"

"Yes, how did you know?"

"That gentleman leaving was Dudley Widworthy. He told us a very interesting tale." WPC Knowle smiled at Ella. "I'm sure Frank will fill you in later."

"Good," said Ella, "That leaves three. Dudley Weston."

Frank jumped in. "Dudley Musbury."

"You know about them all, don't you?"

"Yes, who's the last one?"

"Dudley Gosford-Feniton."

"Correct. We've got him on our list as well."

"Don't tell me. Our letters of complaint were copies. You found the originals in the files."

"You're spot on. Thanks to you and Mrs. Aylesbeare, we've all discovered that there are four Dudleys. Each one of them has complained in writing about Mr. Buckerell in some form or another."

"Four suspects. The Dudleys of Budleigh!"

"There is a fifth suspect, you know?" WPC Knowle was consulting her notebook.

"Yes, of course, the doctor."

Frank added, "He may have been giving Anthony vitamins, but he could also have poisoned him."

"Somehow on that day, someone got to Anthony and poisoned him." PC Hydon stated the obvious.

"Even though he never left your side."

"And that he was in a locked room in the last two hours before he died."

"And that he had a police officer and me as witnesses."

"And that there was an eagle-eyed policeman on guard at the door of the police station. No-one came past me. No-one got in!"

Ella concluded. "Despite all that, someone poisoned him. If it wasn't one of you three, then it could well have been either of the Dudleys or the doctor. Somehow!"

Mrs. Aylesbeare giggled. "You need to see the doctor."

Ella joined in with her giggling and it lightened the situation. The two police officers had other work to do so Frank and Ella volunteered to see Doctor Daniel Moore. Mrs. Aylesbeare told them where the surgery was in Budleigh. It was within walking distance, so they left their car and sauntered up the High Street. Within ten minutes they were in the reception area of the modern-looking medical centre.

There was a queue to speak to the receptionist. Ella stared at the notice board. There were a few local events alongside the usual National Health adverts. One poster held her attention. It was the local amateur dramatic society's latest production of Table for Four. It starred Daniel Moore. At least, it would have done. The word CANCELLED was scrawled at an angle across the poster.

"We ought to start going to the local theatre, Frank."

"You mean the Manor Pavilion Summer Season?"

"Yes, but there are local productions as well."

"Not that one," he said, pointing at the poster.

They reached the front of the queue.

"Hello," began Frank, "We'd like to make an appointment to speak to Doctor Daniel Moore. It's not a medical matter, but more of an urgent personal situation. Is he free?"

The receptionist looked up at them both with a sympathetic smile on his face. "Sorry, sir. Sorry, madam. He isn't here today."

Ella broke in. "Will he be in tomorrow? It's quite important that we..."

The receptionist firmly replied, "Madam, he's not here for the next ten days."

"Oh, do you know how we could contact him?"

"Leave a message with us and we'll pass it on to him when he gets back."

"Where is he?"

"Thailand."

Ella's expression displayed her surprise. "Where?"

"Thailand. On holiday. He left about a week ago and he'll be back at work Monday week. He goes there every year, regular as clockwork."

"Oh, thank you."

"No problem. Did you want to leave a message?" The receptionist held out a message pad and pen to Ella.

"No, we'll come back when he's here again."

"That was quick!"

"Yes, and it puts him out of the picture. According to the receptionist, he left to go on holiday, two days before Anthony Buckerell died."

"I think, being on holiday in Thailand is a very convincing alibi!"

They began walking back to the solicitor's office and their car.

"What do we do now?"

"I think we need to find out more about the four Dudleys."

"Well, Mrs. Aylesbeare helped us with that. She filled us in on the complaints levelled against Anthony Buckerell. That was just before Dudley Widworthy arrived.

"I'm assuming you had a good chat with this Dudley Widworthy?"

"Yes, he told us a fascinating story about bankruptcy and herbal medicines. Dudley was an importer of exotic plants. When we questioned him about poisonous plants, he exploded and stormed out of the office."

"I know, we met him on the stairs. PC Hydon suggested Dudley went back up and apologised."

"It takes a big man to defy PC Hydon!"

"And Dudley Widworthy wasn't that man!"

Frank and Ella went home, not quite knowing what to do next. Their quandary was resolved by a phone call from WPC Knowle. The body of Mr. Buckerell had been released and his funeral was to be held at St Peter's Church on the next Thursday. This was one funeral Frank and Ella were going to attend. No more loitering in the cafe on the other side of the road.

Ella phoned Mrs. Aylesbeare to tell her of their intentions.

"Lovely, Mrs. Raleigh. It'll be good to see you. Come and sit by me if you wish."

"We'd love to," replied Ella. "Who's been doing all the arrangements?"

"Well, actually, I've been trying to do them. It's all been a little bit of a trial." Mrs. Aylesbeare seemed upset and somewhat overwhelmed. "Mr. Buckerell was never blessed with a family. I never heard him speak about his parents. I assumed they'd died a long time ago. He never mentioned any brothers or sisters."

"Has nobody come forward to offer any help?" Ella was saddened to hear Mrs. Aylesbeare's comments.

"No. Not a single soul."

"Let me help you. Two heads are better than one."

"Oh, that would be lovely. Thank you."

"Have you arranged any post-funeral refreshments?"

"Well, yes. As a matter of fact, I found two envelopes in the safe. One contained Mr. Buckerell's will. I put that back into the safe. The other envelope contained his specific funeral instructions. It was all very clear. I've just been following his wishes."

"Excellent."

"Why don't you come around tomorrow morning and we can go through all the arrangements." Mrs. Aylesbeare hesitated. Quietly she added, "I'd appreciate the help."

"Of course. At the office?"

"Yes. About ten o'clock. We can pop into Earls for some coffee."

"See you tomorrow!"

Ella put the phone down feeling she was doing somebody some good. Frank was not so positive.

"Be careful. A woman could administer poison as well as any man. A little old lady like Mrs. Aylesbeare might easily go undetected. She may have been able to get close to Anthony Buckerell. He wouldn't have thought twice about her bringing him a letter to sign or something."

"Perhaps while he was being driven around Dartmoor?"

"Well..."

"I suppose she could have ambushed the police car and injected him with poison while they were stopped for a cream tea. She could have cycled there with the poison in her front basket. Perhaps she met them in Widecombe, or even better, in Princetown!" Ella laughed. Anyway, she could have killed him any number of times. Why choose to wait for him to be surrounded by police?

Frank realised he was losing the thread of his argument. "Perhaps not. But still, be careful."

"I will. I think she's just a lovely old lady who was doing a wonderful job of keeping Anthony Buckerell functioning as a local solicitor. "

Ella was right. Mrs. Aylesbeare - Alice to her friends - was meticulous in her organisation but needed a companion to suggest what needed to be done. Ella considered that to be one of her strengths. Frank called it one of her many super-powers. Together, Alice and Ella made a list. When the list was completed to Ella's satisfaction, then Alice took over. By lunchtime, they were in Earl's enjoying a well-earned cup of coffee and slice of cake.

"Strange to think that this used to be a bank."

"Really?"

"I think the Bank Manager's office was just about where we are now sitting."

"I suppose this was Mr. Buckerell's local branch back then?"

"Yes, it was. How did you know?"

"I just thought that it was probably the closest to the office."

"Absolutely."

They sat quietly finishing their cake and coffee.

"Thank you, Ella, for your help this morning. Without you, this funeral would not be taking place."

"I'm not sure how to take that!"

"No, I didn't mean you killed him. I meant... oh, you know, what I meant."

"Yes, I do, Alice."

They left on the best of terms.

"If you any more help, then just give me a ring. If not, I'll see you at the church."

Frank and Ella were expecting the funeral atmosphere to be sober and solemn. The church was not full but surprisingly well populated. Mrs. Aylesbeare pointed out the Mayor, the Town Clerk and a few councillors.

The coffin was brought in draped in the appropriate flowers - white lilies and two red wreaths. The vicar welcomed everyone to St Peter's. The service would be celebrating the life of a dearly departed friend and colleague.

The Day Thou Gavest, Lord, is ended was sung or mumbled. The mayor stood up, walked to the lectern and proceeded to read Psalm 23. "Yea, though I walk in the valley of the shadow of death."

After a suitable silence, the vicar asked if anybody wished to come to the front and share any memories of Anthony Buckerell. Frank was shocked to see Dudley Widworthy shuffle down the aisle and turn and face the congregation. "This'll be fun," he breathed to Ella.

"I've known Anthony for many years. He was a good friend to me. Often times he offered me sound advice and encouragement. I will miss his solid presence around the town. The place will not seem the same without him." Dudley turned towards the coffin. "Goodbye, old friend."

Dudley then shuffled back to his pew with tears in his eyes. Ella whispered back to Frank, "I wasn't expecting that!"

Another man walked to the front.

"Dudley Gosford-Feniton," hissed Mrs. Aylesbeare.

He turned towards the vicar and asked, "If I may, could I read a poem?"

"Certainly."

"This is a poem by a priest called Henry Scott-Holland. It was part of a sermon he preached in 1910 at St Paul's Cathedral when King Edward the Seventh was lying in state."

Dudley cleared his throat and in a clear dramatic voice recited the famous poem.

"Death is nothing at all.

It does not count.

I have only slipped away into the next room.

Nothing has happened.
Everything remains exactly as it was.
I am I, and you are you,
and the old life that we lived
so fondly together is untouched, unchanged.
Whatever we were to each other, that we are still."

The poem went on and the whole congregation were visibly moved.

Dudley recited the last line "How we shall laugh at the trouble of parting when we meet again!"

Frank was certain he could hear some sniffs and blowing of noses. He turned to look at Ella and Mrs. Aylesbeare and noticed that both had tears trickling down their faces. He glanced around and was quite astonished to observe that they were not, by any means, the only ones.

Dudley Gosford-Feniton bowed his head towards the coffin and slowly walked back to his place.

There was a silence as a number of the attendees sought to recover their composure. There was a scuffling followed by murmurs of "Excuse me." Another gentleman lumbered towards the front. He was rather scruffily dressed. His black suit was ill-fitting and, as he passed, Frank could see that his white shirttails were sticking out.

"Right. I hadn't seen Tony for a few years, not since Vanessa moved to New Zealand. But he was a good bloke. I remember he was a bit of a laugh… on his day. I expect a lot of us will miss the old codger. God bless his soul."

And with that, he shuffled back to his row, mumbled "Excuse me" as he pushed past several seated persons. Eventually, he sat down and bowed his head.

"Who was that?" Ella muttered to Mrs. Aylesbeare.

"I think that was Dudley Weston."

"All we need is Dudley Musbury!" Frank murmured.

"Speak of the devil!" gasped Mrs. Aylesbeare, as a round-shouldered individual in a tweed suit meandered forward. "We'll see some fireworks now," she added.

She was wrong.

"Anthony Buckerell was a gentleman who was misunderstood by some and appreciated by others. He was the epitome of the small-town solicitor. We may never see his kind again. I'm sure we will all miss his knowledge of the law and his clear, cogent and concise arguments and functional advice. He had an effect on so many of us over the years. He certainly affected my life."

The service ambled to a close. The coffin and congregation shuffled out of the church. Then, the coffin was driven away in a sparkling black hearse to St Peter's Burial Ground up near the school. A convoy of cars followed. Frank and Ella stood back to allow local attendees to pay their respects. Standing near the back of the group of mourners, they were well-positioned to hear some illuminating comments.

"Thank heavens, that's over."

"Good riddance to bad rubbish."

"At least there's eats and drinks back at the public halls."

"Bet he didn't pay for it."

"What an absolute mess. First, the cat dies eating some of my special plants. And now, Anthony kicks the bucket."

"Silver lining. More disposable income."

"At least the good doctor gets his starring role."

"I wonder how many of us here are glad to be rid of him?"

"Almost all of us, I expect."

"Was he blackmailing you as well?"

"What do you think?"

CHAPTER 7
A WAKE, A WALK AND A TALK

The wake took place back in the middle of town in one of the rooms at the Public Halls. Alice Aylesbeare and Ella had found a local couple who catered for similar occasions. When they walked in, just ahead of the other mourners, they found everything to be perfectly ready.

"Oh, how excellent. You've done a marvellous job," Alice remarked with a smile to the caterers.

"I'm glad you like it, Mrs. Aylesbeare."

Any further conversation was cut short by the arrival of the main body of mourners. The atmosphere was less sombre than at the church. In fact, it veered towards the jovial. Both Frank and Ella heard some bursts of laughter. The mayor didn't stay too long but thanked everyone for coming and wished them a safe journey home.

"We wanted to make sure he was dead and buried in the ground," someone nearby Frank murmured.

Alice played the part of the convivial hostess making sure everyone was cared for. Frank was startled to notice WPC Knowle standing over the other side of the room, not in uniform, but still formally dressed. She was in earnest conversation with several dignified gentlemen. There were frequent nods and shaking of the heads.

In his meanderings around the room, Frank heard some further comments which were at odds with the public utterances in church.

Slowly but steadily, the mourners declined in numbers. Some people thanked Mrs. Aylesbeare for her hospitality, others just walked out of the door.

Soon it was Frank, Ella and Mrs. Aylesbeare helping the caterers to clear up.

"I know I shouldn't say it, but I'm glad that's over," sighed Mrs. Aylesbeare.

"You did a marvellous job, Alice."

"With your indispensable help."

At last, everyone was cleared up. The caterers bade farewell and Mrs. Aylesbeare thanked them for their hard work and promised to pay them as soon as she received their invoice. "You were brilliant. I'll recommend you to anyone who needs catering!"

Frank and Ella asked if there was anything else that needed doing.

"No, I'll lock up and return the key to the council office."

"Goodbye, then."

"Are you going to continue your investigations?"

"That depends upon WPC Knowle. If she says so, then I'm sure we'll be seeing more of each other."

"I do hope so."

"We need a walk," said Frank the next morning, "The weather looks set for a fine day."

"We also need to learn a bit more about Budleigh Salterton. You know, until this past week, we've never spent much time there."

"Then the obvious thing to do is to go for a walk in Budleigh Salterton!"

"You consult the oracle and I'll check out my walking boots."

Frank went to his computer and found the South West Coast Path website.

"I've found us the perfect walk. West Down Beacon."

"Go on," said Ella.

"It starts in Budleigh at the Public Hall and goes up to the old railway line, through woodland, over a golf course and back into Budleigh from West Down Beacon along the Coast Path."

"How far is it?"

"Almost four miles."

"Excellent. A couple of hours in the sunshine and sea air. We can do the walk and then wander around Budleigh and see if we can find a bite to eat."

Frank and Ella were soon ready. They drove to Budleigh and parked in the free car park behind the Public Hall. Boots were tied. Frank had packed his rucksack with the bare essentials - a jumper each if the wind gathered strength and a couple of apples for a snack.

They set off across the park alongside Station Road and headed up Moor Lane. "This is the way to the cemetery, isn't it?" asked Ella.

"Yes. Was it only yesterday? Strange how so many people said one thing in public and quite another in so-called private chatter."

"Well, they didn't seem to mind being overheard."

Frank mused on the comments he had heard. "You know, a lot of them mentioned blackmail."

"That's got to be worth investigating."

They passed the cemetery and the school and made their way up Bedlands Lane. Reaching the main road between East

Budleigh and Knowle, they crossed and headed up Bear Lane. They both were highly amused by the signpost to Pooh Corner.

"And every one of the Dudleys got up to offer their condolences." Ella continued their dissection of the funeral conversations.

"Speaking very highly of him into the bargain!"

"Most peculiar."

"Yet again when we ask questions, it'll be interesting to hear their reasons."

"Do you think they've been collaborating?"

"You mean, they're all in it together?"

"Once more, worth investigating."

By this time Frank and Ella had reached the Budleigh to Exmouth Cycleway which runs along the site of the old railway line. The railway used to run from Tipton, through Newton Poppleford and Otterton before passing by Budleigh Salterton and then chugging down to Exmouth.

Frank read from his phone's browser. "This line was built in 1899 and took four years to build. They used two steam navvies which were steam shovels to cut a path through Knowle Hill, one employed at each end of the cutting. They met in the middle."

"Was it popular? Did it carry tons of holidaymakers?"

"I don't think so. It says that by the 1950s it was hardly used."

"I bet Doctor Beeching closed it down!"

"Correct. The last train ran in 1967. By 1998 it was a cycleway. Lord Clinton performed the opening ceremony. He is a relative of Lady Gertrude Rolle."

"Who's she?" Ella smiled.

"She was the honorary driver of the first train that ran from Tipton St John to Budleigh in 1897."

"Small world."

They entered the cutting that the navvies had built passing under the Budleigh road bridge. The occasional cyclist and dog walker passed them, each greeting them with a cheery "Hello!"

"I still can't get used to people's friendliness. They would never greet you like this when we were working back in the rat race!"

"No! Although the way we've joined up with the police, we might yet find ourselves working once more!"

They passed under the Castle Lane bridge before doubling back on themselves as they climbed a short path on their left back to Castle Lane.

Cars were parked at the side of the road. Dog walkers rendezvous. They turned right and walked along Castle Lane before forking left up a footpath. It led them to the golf course. They followed strict instructions - courtesy of the golf club - to stay on the path and not wander onto the fairways. The course was pleasantly active. The occasional cry of "Fore" caused both Frank and Ella to wince. Being hit by a speeding golf ball was not their idea of pleasure! They stopped under the protection of a tree and waited until the nearest players had passed them by.

"Frank, is that one of the Dudleys?"

"Yes, it's that one with the double-barrelled name."

"Dudley Gosford-Feniton."

He walked close by and Ella smiled at him and said "Lovely poem and so well-read. Thank you."

"Pardon?"

"At the funeral. It's always been one of my favourite poems. Although I always thought it was written by WH Auden. Seems I was wrong."

"Yes, you were."

Frank chipped in. "Can we have a word with you sometime soon? We're helping Mrs. Aylesbeare sort out some of Mr. Buckerell's files."

"Yes, and your name came up a couple of times," Ella added.

"We'd appreciate your viewpoint on one matter in particular."

"Certainly, I've nothing to hide. Call me, I'm in the telephone directory. I'm free, the day after tomorrow."

"Excellent!"

"But now, I'm involved in a very important game of golf. Please excuse me."

Dudley Gosford-Feniton and his golf trolley strolled off in the direction of the putting green towards the other three players who were waiting patiently.

"Come along, Dudley. No business allowed on the fairways. You know that."

"It wasn't business. Just some acquaintances of a friend of mine."

Frank and Ella followed the path as it left the golf course and headed through the bracken towards the cliff-top of West Down Beacon. They reached the Coast Path, turned left and headed along the path back towards Budleigh Salterton.

Frank read from his phone again. "There was a fire beacon here, hence the name of West Down Beacon. Then during the Napoleonic Wars, it played the role of a signal station. They used an optical telegraph, which needed a direct line of sight with the previous and next beacons. To the west was Dawlish Head and to the east Peak Hill."

"Don't remind me of Peak Hill!" Ella put her hands over her ears to block out Frank's voice.

Frank stopped reading and continued walking. A while later, as the path started to go downhill Frank continued, "They even used the signal stations to warn of suspected smuggling activities. If they helped catch the smugglers, the signal operators were entitled to a share of the booty!"

Ella was listening once more as they walked in single file, down towards Budleigh.

"Did they use Morse Code?"

"No, they used a system of flags and balls. The different combinations all meant something. One ball above a flag meant enemy frigates were around. Three balls above a flag meant an enemy vessel close to the land."

"They must have been quite a size to be seen out at sea."

"Eventually, the system was replaced with a semaphore telegraph. That was a high pole with hinged signal arms. We did flag semaphore in the cubs when I was a lad."

"Guess who invented that?"

"Baden Powell?"

"No, the French during the Napoleonic Wars!"

They passed through a green field before reaching Budleigh promenade. They were presented with a glorious view of Budleigh, the pebble beach stretching to the estuary of the River Otter. The iconic trees stood there as if protecting the estuary from unwanted invaders.

"Beautiful," murmured Ella as she stood and took in the view.

Frank just nodded.

After a while, they strolled downhill towards the centre of town. They turned off the Coast Path and soon reached the high street. There they found a quaint teashop where they stopped for a leisurely well-prepared meal.

"Lovely day," murmured Ella when they arrived back at the car.

Frank phoned Dudley Gosford-Feniton to confirm their appointment with him. Eleven o'clock at his house in

Budleigh. Two days later at precisely eleven o'clock Frank and Ella parked in the gravel driveway that led to a very imposing Georgian style building.

"Very posh," remarked Ella.

"A late Victorian replica," Frank clarified.

"Are you sure?"

"Speak with confidence and fools will believe you tell the truth!"

"Then it's not late Victorian!"

"Phone App working?"

"Yes. Ready to be switched on!"

"Fully charged?"

"Of course!"

Ella rang the old-fashioned doorbell, and, after a short wait, the door opened and Dudley invited them in.

The inside was as grand as the exterior. There was even a polished stone staircase that angled its way upstairs. Paintings of exotic plants and jungle-like scenery hung in ornate frames on the buff-coloured plaster walls. Everything was quite tastefully presented.

Dudley led them into the sitting room at the front of the house. "Please sit down. Make yourselves comfortable. Coffee?"

"That would be lovely," replied Ella.

Dudley had already prepared refreshments on a hostess trolley. He poured out black coffee in small china cups before adding warm milk.

"Sugar?"

"No thank you, for either of us."

"Very wise."

He passed them their cups and then offered them a plate of very sugary shortbread.

"How can I help you?"

Frank began. "I assume you know how Anthony Buckerell died?"

"It's been in the local papers."

"Indeed. We've been working with the police and the family estate to establish any potential lines of enquiry."

Ella joined in. "We read your letter of complaint."

"Ah yes, I thought that would come out at some point."

Frank continued, "About some inheritance?"

"Yes. I'm sure you'll soon discover the truth so I..."

"Why don't you tell us all about it, Mr. Gosford-Feniton?" Ella asked, rather needlessly. "I'm going to record the rest of our conversation - if you don't mind. I'd be quite happy to provide you with a copy later."

"Yes, that's OK. I understand. It all started many years ago."

"I came to you in good faith, Anthony. I thought you were my friend, not just my solicitor."

"Well Dudley, I am. It's just that you have not been quite straight with me, have you?"

"What do you mean?"

"Well, I've looked into the birth certificate you provided. It's fake."

"How did...?"

"Auntie Clarissa was not your Auntie. In fact, she was not even a distant relation. You've no right to the inheritance. I've got more rights than you have."

"How?"

"Well, during my research, I found out that Auntie Clarissa was a long-lost cousin, twice removed, of mine."

"But she can't be?"

"She is. I managed to get hold of the birth certificate to prove it. I've submitted my claim and I'm very pleased to let you know that they've accepted my evidence. There doesn't appear to be any other living relations, distant or otherwise."

"You must be mad!"

"No, just very careful with my research."

"You won't get away with it."

"There's no question of getting away with it. It's all legal and above board. Anyone can see the facts for themselves. And speaking of facts, your birth certificate and various copies of it are safely stored away in various places."

"You swine, that's…"

"Blackmail? Were you about to say blackmail? That's an interesting word. I was thinking, as a gesture of your appreciation of me not going to the police and the University authorities, you might like to, willingly, pay my subscription to the Golf Club. They've invited me to become a member. It's a bit of an expensive luxury, but…"

"Blackmail!"

"..if you're paying, willingly, of course, then I can afford it."

"Blackmail!"

"No, your kindness towards your friendly local solicitor is most touching and greatly appreciated."

"I should beat you to within an inch of your life."

"I wouldn't advise that. If anything happens to me, I've left instructions to pass a message on to the relevant authorities. I'd make sure you lost your job, your house and your pension!"

I got up to leave.

"I'll send you my bill. Along with the bank details for the Golf Club subscription. Oh, and by the way, the next time I'm up for a part in one of your silly little pantomimes, don't go running to the director..."

I've never slammed a door so hard in all my life.

"I wrote a letter of complaint so, at least, there was a record of my disgust. I didn't and couldn't mention too much about why I was so disgusted, but anyone could read between the lines if they knew him."

"Did you pay the subscription?" Ella gently questioned.

"To my utter shame, I paid every year. However, every time I paid, I wrote another letter of complaint. Again, nothing too lurid, but just enough to build up an irritating portfolio."

"And what about the silly little pantomimes?"

"We're both in the local dramatic society. I saw him there a couple of days ago. He looked his usual rambunctious self. Anyway, I write plays and the annual Christmas pantomime. I even direct a few of our efforts. After his blackmail, I made sure he never got a part that made him look good in the eyes of the audience. Petty, I know, but it was about the only time where I held the upper hand between us!"

Ella smiled when she really wanted to laugh out loud.

"I'm not proud of myself, but..."

"What did he mean about the university authorities?" Frank wanted to find out more about his background.

"I work for Exeter University. I'm a Professor of Tropical Botany. I specialise in African plants."

"How fascinating," interrupted Ella, playing the part of the gushing female.

"Yes, it's been my life's work. I still go to Africa on expeditions to find new varieties and new species. Once I was collecting plants in Tanzania when a herd of elephants came wandering my way."

"Do you mean plants that can be used for medical uses?"

"Yes, but my interest is far wider than just medicinal herbs and plants. I suppose, if I had any particular specific expertise, it would be in the area of…."

"Poison?" guessed Ella.

"This herd of eleph… Yes, how did you know?"

"Just a lucky guess."

CHAPTER 8
IT'S THE QUIET ONES THAT CAUSE THE DAMAGE

Well, that was illuminating. Another one interested in plants."

"And poisons."

Frank and Ella were driving home having parted company with Professor Dudley Gosford-Feniton. Ella had enjoyed their visit and bombarded the professor with a variety of questions about his work.

"I liked him. I do hope he's not our murderer. Not only did he lose an inheritance, but he was reminded about it every time the demand for the golf club annual subscription landed on his doormat."

"Yes, he was being blackmailed. He does know about poisons. But did he have the opportunity?"

"We've got to find out more about how Anthony Buckerell died."

"Did someone poison him during the day?"

"Or at the police station?"

"I can't believe anyone could have got at him in that cell."

"We were locked in. There were no windows. He had no visitors. Yet, somehow he died."

"Perhaps you did it!" Ella chuckled.

"Perhaps I did."

"Don't be silly. You know nothing about poisoning. My cooking is not that bad!"

"No, perhaps I killed him without even realising it. Perhaps it was WPC Knowle. It could have been like that case in Salisbury with the poison in the perfume spray."

"Did either of you spray the room with anything?"

"No. Well, not as far as I'm aware."

The conversation ceased and a thoughtful silence occupied the car until they arrived back in Otterbury.

That afternoon Frank phoned WPC Knowle. He told her about their visit to the professor. He could hear her busily scribbling down some notes as he spoke. Frank mentioned the idea about the perfume spray.

"What do you mean? Like Salisbury?"

Frank explained, "Could we have unwittingly passed on some poison to Mr. Buckerell without us even knowing?"

"I don't see how. Surely we would have died as well?"

"Good point. Is there any news about the type of poison used to kill him?"

"Not yet. I'll get on to them and find out what the hold up is."

"What do we do next?"

"Well, both PC Hydon and myself are too busy on other cases to do any sleuthing but I suggest you find a way to have a conversation with the remaining two Dudleys."

"What about Doctor Moore?"

"I checked on him. He's still on holiday in Thailand. I'll speak to him as soon as he gets back."

"Right, Ella and I will speak to the two other Dudleys and then, I think, we'd better get together and brainstorm a bit."

"Good idea. Give one of us a ring when you're ready to meet."

The next morning Ella popped into Budleigh to meet up with Mrs. Aylesbeare.

"Good morning, I hoped you were still here."

Mrs. Aylesbeare was sat at her desk in the deceased solicitor's office. She was surrounded by papers and files.

"I've been paid till the end of the month so I'm making sure that whoever takes this on has a tidy and organised filing system."

"Whoever takes it on?"

"Mr. Buckerell has no relatives as far as I can find out."

"Not even a distant aunt?"

"No, no-one. Oh, except his wife, but she's in New Zealand. Ex-wife now. I contacted her straight away and she wants nothing to do with the business or the money."

"Really?"

"Yes, and then I checked his will and she's not even in it."

"Oh, that's sad."

"He deposited the will in the safe. I didn't even know it was there until I began sorting this lot out. He wasn't particularly friendly with any other solicitors in the area, so, in the directions for his funeral, he asked me to be the executor. If I was still employed here, that is."

Ella smiled reassuringly.

"Well, I am. Still employed. So, I am his executor."

"Good for you." Ella took her coat off and found a chair in which to sit down.

"Who benefits from the will?"

"I can't tell you until the will is officially read. Sorry. As an executor, I must abide firmly by the protocol."

Ella nodded her agreement.

"Yes, but the will is incredibly interesting. Especially to any detectives trying to solve a murder."

"What do you mean?"

"Oh, sorry! I'm blabbing too much. Forget I said anything."

Ella found some law magazines and began leafing her way through whilst contemplating how interesting the will might be. Mrs. Aylesbeare went back to her paperwork. After a minute or so, she put a rather large and heavy file down and turned back towards Ella.

"You haven't asked me the most obvious question yet."

"And what would that be, Alice?"

"Did I poison Mr. Buckerell?"

"Did you?"

"Well, I had the opportunity. I had the motive. He could be the most infuriating employer sometimes. Every day, I could have slipped something in his coffee."

"So did you kill him?"

Mrs. Aylesbeare laughed. It was a sweet vibrating laugh that suited her little old lady's persona perfectly.

"No, my dear. Mind you, if it had been me, I'd have poisoned his morning cup of coffee years ago."

"How?" Ella raised an eyebrow.

"Deadly Nightshade. They used to call it Belladonna because drinking the juice diluted in water would dilate the pupils and make the lady appear attracted to her lover. Of course, eating a single leaf would cause death. I didn't feed Mr. Buckerell any leaves. He wasn't a salad type of man."

Ella put down the magazines and gave Alice her full attention.

"As I said, I only found out about the will the other day when sorting through the safe. Normally he wouldn't let me anywhere it - the safe that is. I had to phone the makers to get it open. They sent one of their engineers. He used some sort of a passkey or something. I had to sign a lot of very important paperwork before they showed me how to open the thing. Then he only let me open it if he witnessed me doing it."

"Very thorough then?"

"Yes, and then he took photos of each item in the safe."

"This engineer was actually from the company?"

"Oh yes, he asked me to phone the company to make sure. I did, and he was!"

"Fascinating!"

Ella was suddenly reminded of why she had come to see Alice in the first place. "Alice, we need to find a reason to visit Dudley Weston and Dudley Musbury. Can you help?"

"Of course, I can. Now. Let me think?"

Quickly, Mrs. Aylesbeare tapped an index finger on the desk. "The will. You need to go to see them as representatives of the executor to explain the time and venue for the reading of the will."

"Excellent idea. Can you set up appointments for us with them? We're available any morning."

"Leave it with me. I'll phone them, set it all up and then let you have their addresses. That'll make it official!"

"Can I have copies of their letters of complaint?"

"Certainly. As executor, I can allow that!"

"Thank you."

"Do you think one of the Dudleys poisoned him?"

"Yes, but I don't have a clue how."

"You'll find out."

The following Monday Frank and Ella made their way to Dudley Weston's house in Budleigh Salterton. It was situated around the corner from Professor Gosford's-Feniton's luxurious house. Not as grand but it looked more homely.

As they emerged from their car, Frank turned to Ella and asked: "Phone App working?"

"Yes, all switched on!"

"Fully charged?"

"Of course!"

They couldn't see a bell so knocked as loudly as they could on the front door. It was soon opened.

"Come in. Welcome to me 'umble abode!"

He led them into a cosy but dated front room. They all sat down in some surprisingly comfortable armchairs.

"Thank you for seeing us, Mr. Weston. I'm Ella Raleigh and this is my husband, Frank. We're helping Mrs. Aylesbeare who was Mr. Buckerell's secretary."

"Yeah, Mrs. Aylesbeare. Sweet little lady. She phoned."

"Yes, she's the executor of the will and she asked us to help her."

"What d'yer want with me?"

"Mr. Buckerell's will is being read soon and we have been asked to find out if you are willing to attend."

"Me?" guffawed Dudley Weston. "Has the old geezer left me some of his loot?" He laughed and banged his hand on the arm of his chair.

"We're not at liberty to say."

"Why is that so funny, Mr. Weston?" Frank asked.

"Listen, I'm going to tell you a story about Anthony Buckerell and me. Now 'e's gone, it'll do me good to get it all out in the open. He can't get me now!"

"Anthony, what a complete and utter mess."

"You know, I think I'd agree with you."

"Why did Vanessa leave you?"

"Same reason as she left you, I should think. She found something or someone better. With you, it was me. With me, it was the lure of New Zealand. Rugby players, different pace of life, fresh air, mountains, scenery. You name it, New Zealand was the place to be in Vanessa's eyes."

"And you just let her go, without telling me?"

"Of course, she's her own person. She rejected you. She rejected me."

"Rejected is a harsh word."

"But the truth. I wasn't worried. She didn't make too many demands on my money. She left me the house. I paid for her travel and a lump sum to help her get settled. She's done quite well out of me."

"Then why did you go to New Zealand then? To get her back?"

"Certainly not. As she once, quite rightly said, I was married to my profession."

"And money!"

"An indisputable truth."

"Then why did you go?"

"I needed her to sign a few forms. Divorce and finance agreements. Also, you wanted information and, I should think you're very happy with what I provided."

"At a price."

"There's no such thing as a free lunch these days."

"Unless you're a solicitor!"

"That's good. It might also be another truth!"

"Look. Don't think I'm not grateful for the information you gave me. At least, I can write to her again."

"Again?"

"Yes, I don't suppose you knew, but I wrote regularly to her when you were married to her."

Does your charming wife know about your writings?"

"Don't be silly. Doreen would leave me if she found out. She never knew about it. "

"But I did. Vanessa never received any of your flowery letters. I burned them all as soon as they arrived."

"What? How could you?"

"Excuse me, you were writing silly little love letters to my wife. I should think I had every right to dispose of them as I saw fit."

"No wonder she's never written back. I thought it was out of loyalty to you. But you never gave her the opportunity!"

"No, I suppose not."

"And what about the New Zealand address. Was that just made up? Are my letters lying lost in some rural post office mailbag somewhere in New Zealand? No known address?"

"No, that address was correct. Google it and you'll find it."

"Then why hasn't she replied?"

"You'll need to ask yourself that question!"

"You...you...devil."

"Dudley, calm down. I brought your plant seeds back, didn't I?"

"Yes, but I pay through the nose for them."

"Of course. I should think the police and customs would be most interested to question someone who is illegally raising exotic plants that New Zealand has banned from being exported!"

"I should go to the police and let them deal with you. Or,

better still, kill you myself."

"Either way, you'll receive the bigger sentence. I was just the, what do they call it, the mule? The mug? The duped tourist? You were Mister Big."

"Shut up!"

"Careful or I'll have to consider raising the cost of our little arrangement. Speaking of which, I've got another little package here from Vanessa for you. She's very happy to think that I've found a little hobby. She thinks it gives me a break from my profession."

"I think your only profession these days is making money off me!"

"Oh, you should be so lucky. You're not the only iron in my fire! Have you told her about your botanical hobby in your letters?"

"Not yet. I should, though."

"No, you shouldn't. She may start thinking about why and what and who."

"I don't understand?"

"Good, let's keep it that way."

"That was the last conversation we had. I saw him a couple of days before he died but we didn't speak."

"It sounds as if he was blackmailing you?"

"I expect he was. I wish I'd never received any of those stupid packages. I'm gonna make a big bonfire and burn every last one of those wretched Antipodean plants."

"Can we see them before you do?"

"I suppose so. Why?"

"Just interested to see if they flourish in Devon. I suppose it's the same sort of climate as in New Zealand, so they should flourish."

"Yes, of course," Dudley replied rather distractedly, "Follow me."

"Are you able to attend the reading of the will?" Frank asked.

"Abso-bloomin-lutely. It'll be fascinating." The enthusiastic words disguised an air of melancholia.

"I'm sure Mrs. Aylesbeare will be in contact to inform you of the time and the venue."

"It'll be in his office, I reckon."

"Before we go outside, let me give you our phone number. Just in case, you want to speak further." Frank was just about to hand him a card with their phone number on it when he stopped. "No, wait a minute. Let me add Mr. Buckerell's office number as well. Mrs. Aylesbeare will be able to help you if you can't contact us."

"Thanks."

"Lead the way," said Ella.

Dudley Weston left the card on the telephone table in the hallway as he took them out into the compact back garden. In one corner was a small but expensive-looking greenhouse. He unlocked the door and they followed him into a wonderland of greenery. Plants in all stages of development were draped over shelves, on the floor and some even attempting to escape through the air vents in the ceiling. There were a great number of ferns, all sizes, all shapes and every shade of green, brown and yellow that one could imagine. Some exotic coloured flowers stretched towards the artificial lighting spread around the glass walls.

Ella was enthralled. She pointed at one aggressive looking climber. "That one climbing the wooden pole looks as if it could kill! I bet something like that would be quite deadly. "

"No, don't be silly. That's not poisonous. Those climbing plants are all show and no substance. No, it's the quiet ones that cause the damage. It's always the quiet ones. Those two ferns in the corner by themselves. They're really nasty. They did for my poor old cat the other week. She got in and…"

"Oh, how sad!" Ella murmured.

Frank changed the subject and was full of admiration. "My word, it's quite a collection. You must be so proud of them."

"I used to be. But now, it doesn't matter, does it? Nothing matters!"

"Why? Because Anthony's dead?"

"Nah, because I received a letter from New Zealand this morning."

"From Vanessa!" cooed Ella.

"Yes, Vanessa. She was the reason I grew this verdant fern collection of mine. It was my only connection with her. Until I could get her back into my life."

"What about your wife?"

"I don't love her. I never have. Unfortunately, for some reason, she loves me."

"But why destroy it all?"

Vanessa's just married this rugby playing farmer from Waitahuna Gully on South Island. She never wants to hear from me, ever again."

CHAPTER 9
UMBRELLAS AND PHONE CALLS

"Well, that was another strange interview," declared Ella.

"So far, it seems that being on the receiving end of blackmail is becoming a motive for murder."

"Did you notice the plant connection again?"

"Yes, but I still don't understand how they did the murder?"

"We can gather motives and opportunities until the cows come home but if we can't work out how the murder was done…

"You can't charge somebody with murder when a murder hasn't even been committed!"

"Exactly!"

Frank and Ella were sitting at home talking over the interviews and incidents of the past few days. They both felt they were going around in circles. They kept coming back to the question "How do you murder someone who is locked safely away in a police cell with two witnesses alongside them?"

"We're busy going nowhere!"

At that moment the phone rang. Frank and Ella hardly received any calls on their landline phone these days.

Ella got up, with a puzzled expression on her face. She picked up the phone and asked: "Hello, how can I help you?"

The phone had been left on speakerphone from the last phone-call made in the distant past. Frank was able to hear both ends of the conversation.

"That's a laugh! You can't help anyone, can you?"

The voice was a little muffled and disguised. It wasn't even possible to tell if it was male or female.

"Hello, who is this?"

"Call yourself detectives. You couldn't detect a murder when it happens right in front of your face."

"Thank you for your opinion. Who am I listening to?"

"It doesn't matter who I am. I'm not the failure. When I'm finished with you, you'll be the laughing stock of East Devon. I heard about your Cidered in Sidmouth. You got lucky. This time you'll be Baffled in Budleigh! Ha-ha!! Bested in Budleigh. Bamboozled in Budleigh!"

Ella was too shocked to reply. Frank came over to her and took the phone out of her hand.

"Good afternoon, sir."

"Ha! Ha! Ha! Sir or madam? Another guess? You've got a 50 per cent chance of being wrong again!"

"Our phone technology is far more advanced than your brain. Your number has come up on our screen. We'll soon be tracking you down!"

The connection was immediately broken.

"Well done, Frank. That was clever," stumbled Ella, "Have you written the number down?"

"There was no number. It just said number withheld. But they weren't quick enough to realise that."

Ella and Frank went back to their armchair and just sat there trying to calm down and rationalise the past few minutes.

Eventually, Ella sighed, "That was scary? How did someone

get our number?"

"We're in the directory."

"I don't want to be anymore."

Frank nodded and silently promised to look at how they went about becoming ex-directory. They had never needed to think about that before. Even when teaching, no-one had abused the privacy of their home phone number.

"Somebody is worried we're getting close."

"Did it sound like any voice you recognised?"

"No, it was disguised. Someone could have been holding a handkerchief or scarf in front of the phone."

"It sounded more like a tin or a saucepan judging by the echo."

Frank picked up his mobile phone and contacted WPC Knowle. This time, she was able to speak with him. He explained the call.

"Right, next time they call, we'll get them. We've got a voice recorder device that can not only record the call but track down where the call came from - regardless of whether the number is withheld or not. PC Hydon will be around in the morning to set it up. He'll be there at eleven on the dot."

The next day, right on schedule, the voice recorder was fitted. PC Hydon showed both Frank and Ella how it was activated before bidding them farewell. Twenty minutes later, the phone rang. This time it was the grandmotherly tones of Mrs. Aylesbeare. "Hello, Ella. I've just received a very strange call from Mrs. Weston. It seems that Dudley has run away!"

"Dudley Weston? But we were only over there yesterday."

"I know, Mrs. Weston told me. She's not very happy with you two. She thinks you scared him over Mr. Buckerell's death."

"I don't think we even mentioned that he was a suspect."

"Well, she was very annoyed and very loud. She wanted to know where you lived."

"Why?"

"I think she wants a few words with you."

There was a loud knocking at the door.

"You didn't tell her where we lived, did you?"

"Of course not!"

"How did she get your number?"

"I asked that. She said she found it on a card by the telephone."

The knocking continued.

"I'd better go. There's someone at the door!"

"Right, I just thought you should know. Goodbye."

"Goodbye, Mrs. Aylesbeare, er, Alice."

Ella went to the front door, slipped the security chain on and tentatively opened the door a couple of centimetres.

"Parcel delivery."

Ella released the chain and fully opened the door with a sigh of relief.

"Thank you. Do I need to sign?"

Ella related the gist of the phone call to Frank.

"I think we'd better go around to her house. We can explain about our visit and maybe find out more about Dudley."

"I expect he's gone away somewhere to think things over."

The day was cold, so they gathered together coats and gloves and went to the car. As Frank was just reversing the car onto the road, another vehicle screeched to a halt blocking them in. A woman climbed out waving a rolled-up umbrella over her head. She came over to their car and thumped the umbrella menacingly on the roof of their car.

"Get out. Get out. I want a word with you!"

Frank opened the door and caught the umbrella in his hand snatching it away from the woman.

"Mrs. Weston, I presume."

"How did you know?"

"Your reputation proceeds before you."

Ella had emerged from the car and came around to invite Mrs. Weston indoors.

"Do come in. A nice cup of tea and we'll soon sort things out!"

"Why should I? You've done something with him. Have you kidnapped him?"

Frank was astounded "Mrs. Weston, I can assure you…" That was as far as he got. Mrs. Weston looked as if she was going to grab her umbrella back and use it on him.

"Mrs. Weston," Ella shouted in an authoritative voice, "Do come in and Frank will make you a nice cup of tea. Unless you want a coffee?"

"No, tea'll do."

Ella directed Mrs. Weston through the front door that Frank had opened. She shooed Frank towards the kitchen whilst anxiously whispering "How did she get our address?"

Then Mrs. Weston and Ella went and sat down in the front room.

"Isn't it a beautiful view, Mrs. Weston?"

"Yes, is that Mutter's Moor?"

"It is indeed. And there's Fire Beacon Hill."

"Yes, lovely."

"Now, how can we help you?"

Mrs. Weston appeared calmer as she took in the panoramic

view from the window.

"It's my Dudley. What have you done to him?"

"Nothing, Mrs. Weston, absolutely nothing."

"But you came around yesterday and after you'd gone, he wasn't the same."

"We said nothing to cause him any concerns. Are you sure it was our visit that upset him? Was he any different after we went or was he upset before we arrived?"

"Now you mention it, there was something wrong with him all day."

"Interesting."

Frank came in with the tea and biscuits on a tray. Never had refreshments been prepared so quickly. He didn't want to miss a word. Mrs. Weston accepted a cup of tea and a malted milk biscuit. She needed to talk. So, she did.

"He spent the afternoon at his desk in the study. He didn't say a word during our evening meal. After that, he said he was going to the pub. We normally go together. I don't like him spending all his time there, drinking and whatever."

"Is he a bit of a drinker, then?"

"No, not at all. But I like to keep an eye on him. Just in case."

"So, he went to the pub without you?"

"Yes, and he took the car. We normally walk. Saves on the petrol."

"What time did he come back?"

"That's just it. He didn't."

"I walked down at about half-past eight to see if how he was. I suppose I wanted to make sure he hadn't drunk too much and then got into the car to drive home. Heaven knows what might have happened."

"He wasn't there, was he?" said Ella.

"No, he hadn't been there all evening. And he never came

home later. His bed wasn't slept in this morning."

"Has he phoned?"

"No."

"Have you called the police?"

"Yes. I explained the situation, but they said they'll have to wait till he's been missing for over twenty-four hours."

"How did you find where we lived?"

"I saw your card on the telephone table yesterday and copied down the numbers. I did a Google search and found out how to do a reverse lookup. If you'd given Dudley your mobile number, I'd never have found your address."

"Very clever!"

Frank made a mental note to never give out his land-line phone number ever again! In fact, it might be a good idea to just get rid of it.

"Why do you think he might have gone?"

"He was upset. Something happened. He was so much happier these past few weeks. He went to that funeral with his friends and then it was as if a black cloud had been lifted off his shoulders."

"Mr. Buckerell's funeral?"

"I think that was his name? But then yesterday, it was like the black cloud descended again."

She stared out of the window munching a biscuit.

"Is he out there all on his own? What am I going to do without him?"

"It's too early to worry like that. There's must be plenty of reasons why he stayed out the night." Ella was aware she hadn't phrased that in a very caring manner. It may have opened up some unwanted trains of thought.

Frank jumped in before Mrs. Weston could say anything. "Was he usually a happy personality?"

"Well, he found it hard to express his feelings. I usually could tell how he was. He never really voiced whether he was happy or sad."

She stared once more out of the window before turning to Ella.

"He never said he loved me, not once, but I know he did. If he doesn't come back, then... I never got the chance to tell him... but I did love him... I do..."

Tears were rolling down her cheeks.

Frank coughed. "Mrs. Weston, we'll find him for you. Does he have a mobile phone?"

"No, he wouldn't know how to use one."

"That might make it more difficult. Look, you go home and make us a list of every friend, every acquaintance of his. Where does he work? Write down his favourite places. Has he got a favourite holiday location? Camping site? Hotel? Write it all down and we'll do some digging."

"I'll speak to the police and voice your concerns. We'll find him. He'll soon be home."

They continued drinking whilst Frank and Ella engaged in some gentle questioning. How long had they lived in East Devon? What job did Dudley do? Did they have any children? The conversation drifted from the mundane to the inane until Mrs. Weston gathered herself together and prepared to leave.

"I'll do what you suggested. I'll phone you when I've gathered my thoughts."

"You've got our number!"

As soon as Mrs. Weston had calmly left to return home, Frank phoned WPC Knowle.

"We've just had a surprising visitor."

Frank went on to recount the recent encounter and then, the details of their conversation with Dudley Weston. As usual, he could hear WPC Knowle furiously scribbling in her notebook.

After Frank had finished and WPC Knowle had stopped writing, she said "Doctor Moore is back with us. I spoke to him yesterday. He started off by saying that he knows nothing about why anyone would want to kill Mr. Buckerell."

"Started off saying?"

"Yes, but the end of our brief conversation, he'd implicated all four of the Dudleys in one way or another."

"Anything new?"

"No. I think we already knew every snippet of gossip that came from his lips."

"And he definitely left the country?"

"Absolutely. He says he left Budleigh three days before Mr. Buckerell died. However, I checked with Heathrow and Dr Moore left for Thailand the day before the death."

"He could have been visiting friends in London or shopping… "

"True. But it's worth storing away the information. Just in case."

"Fair enough. But getting back to Dudley Weston. Mrs. Weston says he was troubled all day. Now he's run away or gone to ground. Can you do anything?"

"I'll go to talk to her and see if we can get a recent photo. We'll circulate it and see what we come up with."

"That would be great."

"However, in most of these cases, the husband just wants a bit of peace and quiet. He probably wants time to think it through."

"She didn't appear to know anything about the blackmail or Vanessa."

"Good. I'll try to keep it that way. It's not my job to stir up unnecessary hurt and pain. I deal with enough of it already without creating any more!"

There was a moment of silence.

"Is that everything? I'll tell Mrs. Weston to give you any ideas she gets about where her husband might be staying. If you find anything, let me know. Don't do anything stupid."

"We won't. We're learning to go softly, softly in this detective profession."

"You're just assisting. If Mrs. Weston gives you any leads, make sure you tell me before you follow any of them up. And if you go on any reconnaissance mission, don't take Mrs. Weston with you. She doesn't seem a very tactful personality! Speak soon."

Frank put the phone down and was pleased to see that the auto voice recorder had clicked in and had recorded all of the conversation. It even showed the number dialled.

Before Frank could go and share his conversation with Ella, the phone rang again. "I'll bet she's forgotten some important piece of info."

"Hello, what did you forget to…"

"Shut up and listen."

Frank recognised Dudley Weston's voice.

"I think I know who murdered Anthony Buckerell."

"Are you at home?"

"Nah, not likely. Get yourself to Staverton. Find the bus shelter near the pub. TTFN."

CHAPTER 10
A NICE CUP OF TEA

"Staverton? Where's that?"

"I've heard of a Staverton Station on the South Devon Railway. Their signal box is a wonderful story!"

"There may be another Staverton?"

Frank turned to Google maps on his iPad. "There's two. One in Northamptonshire near Daventry and one in Devon."

"Is the one in Devon nearby?

"Between Buckfast and Totnes. South Devon. Here you are. Staverton Station is on the South Devon Railway. There must be a pub and a bus shelter there."

"Let's go, then."

"No, wait. There's no bus shelter that I can see. Or a pub."

"How can you see that on a map?"

"I'm using Street View." Ella moved alongside him, so she could see the screen. "There's the station. Level crossing gates then a bridge over the river."

"If that's near Totnes, that must be the River Dart," Ella added.

"Looks like it. If I turn the Street View man around the other way. Aah, yes, there's a signpost. Staverton – half a mile."

"The village is quite a long way from the station?"

"Yes, that often happened. The railway needed level land. The village was there before the railway and if the village wasn't in the valley but nestled amongst higher ground, then the railway could only get so near. I know one village in Herefordshire where the old village died when the railway came. They put the station a mile and a half away. The villagers wanted the railway so much they built houses around the station. The church was left on its own in the old village."

"Whatever, the reason, we need the village and not the station."

"True. I'm going to phone WPC Knowle and let her know what we're doing. I'll leave the iPad to charge up whilst we're out and then I'm ready to go."

Frank phoned WPC Knowle. There was no reply, so he left a quick message. "We're after Dudley Weston. He contacted us and told us to meet him at the bus shelter by the pub. We'll update later."

They set off from Otterbury towards Exeter. They would join the motorway before taking the Plymouth road up Haldon Hill and past the racecourse. Ella drove and Frank navigated. The drive was more hectic than usual. The M5 around Exeter was crowded even though it was nowhere near the tourist season. They chugged up Haldon Hill. When they reached the summit, they waved at Exeter racecourse on their left and kept in the left-hand lane down the A38 dual carriageway. Bovey Tracey and Trago Mills were soon bypassed. Then they were careering down the long straight downhill stretch towards Ashburton. After Ashburton, the road swept around flowing corners until the signpost appeared for the A384 towards Totnes. Ella was glad to get off the main road. She was a good competent driver, but she was always aware that lorries and vans paid scant attention to small cars like hers. They were only concerned with getting from A to B in the quickest possible time.

"What's he doing in Staverton? It's a long way from Budleigh Salterton."

Through the trees, Frank could see the River Dart flowing over rocks in the valley to their right.

"Perhaps he just wanted to get away from his wife."

"Don't you get any ideas!"

"I love my wife. I don't think he loves his!"

The South Devon Railway appeared on their right. For a short while, road and railway ran side by side. Ella saw a bus stop on the left as Frank said, "After the bus stop, turn left for Staverton."

There was no signpost, but Ella indicated and branched off to the left. The road became narrower, passing a farm shop, and winding its way through tall hedges and bare trees towards Staverton. There were few houses but plenty of leafless trees. All at once, they reached Staverton Station. Frank recognised it from Street View. There was no bus shelter or pub. There was a signpost guiding them towards either Staverton or Staverton Bridge.

"Turn left," said Frank. "This way to the village." They left the old station and a well-presented business area behind them, passed a grassed area with a football pitch before reaching the village of Staverton. They ignored a small car park on their right because they could see in front of them the whitewashed walls of a pub.

"There's a bus shelter!" cried Ella. She slowed down and stopped outside the pub. On the apex of the junction was an old wooden bus shelter. The front of it was festooned by posters and adverts.

"Just as he said. Now, where is he?"

Frank and Ella got out of the car and looked around them. There was no-one in sight. The pub looked deserted. It was so quiet that they could hear the train whistle far away in the distance.

"South Devon Railway," murmured Frank.

They crossed the road and went to inspect the bus shelter. Inside the shelter, there were just as many posters and leaflets. One, in particular, jumped out at them. It was a square of bright pink, fluorescent paper. On it, in large capital letters were their names.

"Frank and Ella. Your next clue is at the station."

"Is this some kind of a joke?" voiced Ella.

"Someone is playing a game of Treasure Hunt." Frank smiled, "Let's play along."

He headed back to the car. Ella followed and she drove them back towards the station. This time, they passed over the level crossing and parked the car under some trees. They got out and looked around for a notice board. To their left was a small compact Great Western Railway signal box. It was a single-story building with no outside stairs.

"There's the signal box I was telling you about. It's a wonderful story! The line opened in 1872 but it only lasted 90 years before it closed for good. The Dart Valley Light Railway Company took ownership of the line in 1965. As they were preparing to re-open it, they couldn't find the signal box. They located it eventually in the local vicar's back garden. He'd bought it when the original railway closed down and was using the signal box as a greenhouse."

"With those windows, I could see how it might be mistaken for a greenhouse," laughed Ella.

"Anyway, they bought him a suitable replacement and restored the signal box back into its original place performing its original task."

"A greenhouse," smiled Ella, "now where's our next clue?"

On the brick wall of a large station building was a series of bygone adverts. Stuck to the yellow Woodbine advert was another bright pink piece of paper.

Frank reached up and prized it off the metal advert.

"No writing. Just a map."

It was a hand-drawn map with a couple of direction arrows on it. They recognised the railway, the river and a bridge. They headed back to the car to find another bright pink note attached to the windscreen.

Frank read. "Leave your car here. It's perfectly safe. Time for a walk."

Frank looked around to see if the note placer was still around. Apart from the odd four-wheel-drive passing by, the place looked deserted.

Ella was not happy. "This is getting silly. I don't like it one bit."

Frank smiled. "We've got our walking shoes and stuff in the boot. Let's kit ourselves out and follow the map. What have we got to lose?"

"OK. I hope I don't need to remind you of what you just said." Ella laughed and opened the boot.

They equipped themselves for a short walk. Frank left his rucksack behind. It didn't look like a day for waterproofs.

They could see the sense in leaving the car at the station. They crossed the bridge over the Dart and were soon on a winding footpath which took them through the trees into very dense woodland. They could hear the river somewhere to their left.

Eventually, after fifteen minutes of steady walking, they emerged alongside an old cottage. It was remote, unpainted with moss covering most of the slate roof. The walls were half-covered with ivy. The whole place had the air of being unkempt and uncared for. They were well away from any road, just a muddy track hemmed in by overhanging hedges leading away from the tumbledown building. There was a cramped, empty yard in front of the house. No garden or front gate. Just a wooden, badly painted front door.

On that door was another bright pink square of paper with only one word on it in very large handwritten capitals "Welcome!" The door was slightly ajar.

"I hope this is not an action replay of Sidmouth," whispered Frank.

He pushed the door open. It creaked just like in an old horror movie. Frank stepped cautiously inside. Ella grabbed his hand and followed.

Everywhere was musty, dusty and about fifty years out of fashion. Pine cladding covered one wall. An old bubble lamp stood on top of a pine cabinet. The room smelled damp. An old armchair dozed in one corner of the room. Frank tried the light switch by the door somehow knowing the lights wouldn't come on. They didn't.

The kitchen door was ahead of them. It too was slightly open. There was part of a table in view. Frank and Ella walked slowly towards the room, pushed open the door and saw three mugs of tea on the old wooden table.

"Welcome, come in. I've made you a mug of tea. No sugar, I'm afraid."

They passed through into the kitchen and saw Dudley Weston sitting to one side of the table. He picked up one of the mugs and began drinking.

"You got my messages then?"

"Er, yes," said Ella in a confused voice.

"Well, sit down. Your tea's getting cold."

Both Frank and Ella sat down on old wooden kitchen chairs. They both picked up a china mug and sipped their tea.

"I'm afraid, it's not Tetley's. They only had Lipton's and it was some kind of Indian flavour. It's not to my taste but beggars can't be choosers, can they?"

Frank continued to sip the warm tea. The taste was horrible, but his English upbringing got the better of him. He did think, however, that he should gain some semblance of control in the situation.

"Mr. Weston, er, Dudley, what are you doing here?"

"Escaping from my boring and overbearing wife. Have you met her?"

"Yes, we did," said Ella.

"Then you'll understand my actions!"

Ella thought the tea was an acquired taste and she hadn't quite acquired it yet.

"But why here?"

"Staverton? That's a long story. I'll give you the abbreviated version. We used to come here when I was a child. Mum and Dad loved the area. I loved the steam trains. But more importantly, Doreen doesn't know this place even exists. I came here a couple of years ago on my own exploring. It was run-down but habitable. Over the years, I'd been able to sell a few of my more exotic plants for a tidy profit. I kept the money quiet. The house was cheap, very cheap. I bought it. Doreen never knew."

"Good hideaway," remarked Frank. He'd never felt less in control of a conversation.

"How are you feeling?" said Dudley.

"A bit tired after our walk," Ella replied.

"Good. I brought you here for a reason."

"Brought us here?" Frank was feeling tired as well.

"Yes. You see, I know who murdered Anthony Buckerell. I just need some more evidence and then I'll be turning the culprits over to the police. I bet there's a great big fat reward for assisting the police. I need your help to provide the evidence."

"How?"

"Well, a confession. An explanation of how the murder was done. How the police officers were bribed. Or were they in collusion with the murderers?"

"What are you talking about? I don't understand?" Ella tried to concentrate on his words.

"Of course, you do. Are you feeling sleepy?"

"Yes, I am. Have you put something in our drinks?" Frank knocked the almost empty mug off the table. It smashed on the floor.

"Temper, temper!"

"Have you drugged our drinks?" repeated Frank.

"You're the supposed detective. You tell me?"

Frank tried to stand up, but the effort was too great.

"Wait a moment," interrupted Ella, "you said something about a confession. Have you got the murderer here in this place?"

"I have now." Dudley Weston smiled at Ella in a most disturbingly smug manner.

"Where?"

"Here."

"Who are they?"

"Surely you know. It's you. Frank and Ella Raleigh. You killed Anthony Buckerell and when you wake up, you're going to tell me how and why?"

CHAPTER 11
THAT'S ONE WAY TO STOP A TRAIN!

It was dark and silent when Frank awoke. It took him a couple of minutes to fully understand where he was and how he got there. His head was thumping like a hammer in a blacksmith's forge.

He was in a room with no windows. He couldn't tell whether it was morning, noon or night. For some reason, he was unable to move his hands to be able to see his watch. The whole room smelt of mouldy hay. He couldn't move because although he was sitting up straight, his arms and legs were tied and tightly attached to a wooden kitchen chair. It seemed to be the same chair he had been in when drinking a strong cup of tea. He recalled the taste and his drowsiness. Drugged.

He looked around as far as was possible. His eyes were getting accustomed to the darkness. Tied to another chair was a still sleeping Ella. There was one closed door in the far wall. No chinks of light were visible around the edges of the door frame. The room was bare of furniture but appeared to be partly covered in hay. No wallpaper or paintwork on the walls- just bare bricks. It could be an outhouse or an attic. He couldn't tell.

He heard a scurrying noise near his feet. Mice in the hay?

Rats? He didn't want to think about that! He heard another noise. A moan followed by a groan.

"Frank?"

"I'm here. About six feet away from you. I'm tied up as well."

"Dudley Weston?"

"He's not here. It's just us. How's your head?"

"I've felt better."

There was a rustle.

"I can't move my hands or feet."

"Yes, same here." replied Frank, "We've been tied up rather expertly."

"What do you remember about the kitchen... about his accusation?"

"Now you say that, I do remember. He accused us of murdering Anthony Buckerell. But, that's impossible."

"No, it's not!" A voice resounded loudly from the furthest corner of the room.

"Dudley Weston?"

"Yes, Mrs. Raleigh. I've been waiting patiently for you to wake up. Would you like another cup of tea?" He laughed mockingly.

"Let us out of these ropes. We need to get home."

"No chance!"

"Why keep us here in this cellar?" demanded Frank. "Or is it an attic?"

"If you would just loosen these ropes on my hands. They're hurting me."

"Tough, Mrs. Raleigh."

"Just let us go home and we'll say no more about it," Ella lied. If Ella could have crossed her fingers, then they would all have been crossed.

"You're not going home again for a good number of years."

"What are you going to do with us?" Ella's voice now betrayed a touch of genuine fear.

"Don't worry. I'm not going to exact any revenge. I'll leave that to the powers that be. They'll administer justice. I just want to hear from your own lips how you did it."

"Did what?"

"Don't be so blooming dense, Mr. Raleigh. You both managed to do something that I wished I had the nerve to do. He probably deserved it. But I still want to hear from you. How did you kill him?"

Ella had regained her nerve. "That's strange, Mr. Weston, because I was most interested to hear how you did it."

"What?"

"How did you murder Anthony Buckerell? It must have been you. Or else, why would you run away after we questioned you? That's the actions of a guilty conscience."

"Oh, I see, what you're doing. Trying to deflect your guilt onto me. Well, it won't work. I've got all the time in the world. When you're good and ready, we're gonna record your confession. And then I'm gonna ring the police and tell 'em to come here and arrest you."

"You're going to have a long wait."

There was silence. Then Frank heard some more rustling near where Dudley Weston had been. Suddenly, a bright light shone from there onto his face. Then, another, directly onto Ella's face. It was so bright that neither Frank nor Ella could see anything else in the room.

"Right. Some questions. Firstly, how did he die? Was it really a heart attack or was it poison?"

"You know it was poison," spluttered Frank.

"Correct. How did you administer it? Did you bribe your police officer friends?"

"No bribery because there was no need. I didn't kill him, as well you know."

"Perhaps it was Mrs. Raleigh, then? Was she in the room as well? I read about it in the paper, but they didn't mention your charming wife?"

"I was at home."

"Really?"

"Bella and George came around in the evening. My friends."

"Phone them and check Ella's story," added Frank.

"So, it was just you, then?"

"Don't be so ridiculous, Dudley. You're wasting our time and your time. When the toxicology report comes out, they'll be able to tell us all which poison killed him. The police will be all over your house. They will examine every one of your exotic plants. And if they find a plant that produces the strain of poison that killed Anthony Buckerell, then they will arrest you for murder!"

There was silence from the other side of the room.

"That's given you something to think about, eh?" remarked Ella.

The lights went off and before they could do anything, the door opened, and Dudley Weston left the room.

"Well..." started Frank.

"Sssh, Frank. Listen," whispered Ella.

They strained to hear any noise. There was none.

"He hasn't gone down or upstairs. I don't think this is a cellar or an attic."

"I bet we're on the ground floor."

"I didn't hear a key turn or a bolt slam when he left."

"Useful to know. Are your ropes hurting you?"

"Of course not!"

"How tight are they?"

"Not as tight as they were!"

"Same here. We need to work at loosening them and then prepare an escape plan."

Dudley Weston returned later. It may have been a gap of two hours. Neither Ella nor Frank could tell or cared.

"Brought you some refreshment. Tea and biscuits. I'll leave them here."

He moved a small circular table and placed it between them. He put a tray with mugs of tea and a plate of biscuits on the table.

"We're not hungry." Ella snapped.

"How are we going to eat or drink if you've tied us up?"

"Good point," said Dudley. He laughed. "See you later!"

After he had walked out of the room, they listened, once more, for any clues. No key. No bolt. No footsteps. There was a sound of another door opening and closing.

"He's either gone outside or there's another room."

"Perhaps we're next to the kitchen?"

"I didn't hear a kettle boil."

Again silence.

"How's the loosening going?" Ella asked.

"I'm getting there. Give me another hour or so."

"I'm almost free. My hands are smaller than yours and he didn't tie them that tight in the beginning."

"Keep going, love."

In a few minutes, Frank heard a scraping sound and a whispered cry of "Yes!"

"Success?"

"Like a mobile phone! Hands-free!"

Another sixty seconds dragged by.

"Free!"

"Keep your voice down and come over here and help me."

Ella got up and rushed over to Frank. "Watch the ta…."

Ella collided with the table. The china mugs and plate went flying. The noise was enough to be heard in Totnes. Tea sprayed over Frank. Ice cold tea. They both waited for the inevitable response to the clatter. Incredibly, there was none.

Ella quickly untied Frank. They both stood there, arms wrapped around each other in a desperately thankful hug.

"Time to get out of here."

They opened the door and went stealthily into the kitchen.

"The tea was ice cold. No wonder we didn't hear the kettle."

There were two doors. One the way they had come in through the front room, the other out to the back of the house.

"He may be in the front room," whispered Frank. They left the house through the unlocked back door.

Outside it was daylight but raining, wet mizzly rain that soaked through their clothes in minutes.

"We can't go back through the woods. If he's in the front room, he'll see us."

"He may have gone out. If we go along the track, we may run into him."

"Let's head out through the back. I think we'll be able to reach the river that way."

They steadily made their way through the shallow undergrowth, bushes and small trees that surrounded the back of the house. After a couple of minutes, they were far enough away from the house to be able to stop and listen.

"I don't think he's following us. I think we're going to be okay!"

"Did you hear a car?"

"No. A car couldn't follow us into here."

"I'm not so sure. It's pretty creepy in these woods. It's like the trees have got eyes. "

Ella was spooked.

Frank peered through the gloom. "There looks like a clearing ahead."

They made for it with as much speed as they could muster and stumbled over some metal rails and wooden sleepers. A deafening train whistle behind them caused them to turn towards the source of the sound. Steaming towards them at about twenty-five miles per hour was a 5700 class 0-6-0 Pannier engine. Frank grabbed Ella and vaulted frantically away from the train and onto the sloping ballast at the side of the track.

The train rumbled and screeched to a halt. Both driver and guard jumped down from the train. Incredulous faces stared down from the carriage windows.

"You can't stop the 10.30 from Buckfastleigh to Totnes. It's against regulations!" shouted the driver.

"What in heaven's name were you doing?" shouted the guard, "We almost killed you!"

"I'm sorry," cried Ella. "We've just escaped from a cottage over there." She waved a hand blindly behind her.

"We were kidnapped. Imprisoned."

"You're soaked through. Where's your coats?" asked the driver.

"Thomas, get back to your cab. I'll deal with this."

Thomas grunted to no one in particular. "Well, that's one way to stop a train!" and plodded away back to his cab.

Ella turned towards the guard and held onto the sleeve of his uniform. "Please, take us to the police," she sobbed. "We need them to arrest Dudley. He thinks we're murderers."

"Well, I haven't a clue what you're talking about, but you need to warm up. Come with me to the guard's van. We'll take you to Totnes."

Frank and Ella followed the guard and climbed aboard the train.

"We'll pay for a ticket," Frank volunteered.

"It sounds like that's the least of your problems," laughed the guard. He stuck his head out of the door and waved a green flag.

In a short while, the train jolted and moved slowly forwards on its journey.

The guard picked up a mobile phone and spoke to Totnes Station.

"We've had a bit of a to-do. We've stopped to pick up two sodden people just after Staverton. Luckily, we were still in the vicinity of the station otherwise we wouldn't have been able to stop in time."

He listened to some chatter from Totnes.

"Yes, I think they're genuine. They want to talk to the police."

Again, he listened.

"Oh, that's good."

He turned to Frank and Ella. "They'll be there to meet you at the station."

"Yeah, still here. We'll lament our way towards you." Another short gap. "About thirty-five minutes, Totnes Riverside. Speak to you soon."

He put down his phone and turned back towards the shivering couple.

"Right, here's a warm blanket each. No, make it two. Wrap them around you. Sit here by the fire. Yes, we still have a brazier in the guard's van. Would you like a cup of tea?"

Both Frank and Ella shook their heads. "No, thank you!"

The train rumbled on its way. The warmth of the fire permeated their soaked clothes. The guard made inconsequential chit-chat and Totnes Riverside soon rolled into view.

The train lurched to a halt.

"Just wait until the paying passengers have dismounted. Don't want them to see you all wet and straggly. Not a good advert for Devon weather, even at this time of the year."

Frank and Ella were relieved not to have to walk through a gauntlet of gawping passengers.

The guard's van door opened, and two police officers entered the van. Ella fully expected to see WPC Knowle and PC Hydon. There were female and male but not Elsie and Alf.

"Are you Frank and Ella Raleigh?"

"Yes, we are."

"Well, sir and madam, you are under arrest for the murder of Anthony Buckerell!"

CHAPTER 12
THE THAMACIN REVELATION

Frank and Ella looked at the policeman in stunned silence.

"You've got to be kidding," muttered Ella.

Frank recovered his powers of speech. "We've just been kidnapped, drugged and imprisoned. And you're arresting us?"

"Sir and madam, you do not have to say anything. But it may harm your defence if you do not mention when questioned something which you later rely on in Court. Anything you do say may be given in evidence."

"Yes, we understand, we've heard it before."

Ella, much to her surprise, remained calm. "Look, officers, you've got it all wrong. Can we go to your police station and we'll explain our situation? We'll answer any questions you want to ask us."

"I suppose Dudley Weston has put you up to this."

The female officer raised her eyebrows before replying. "I'm afraid I'm not at liberty to disclose that information."

"You just did," said Frank.

They sat in the interview room at Totnes Police Station. They declined the presence of a solicitor.

"Would you like a cup of tea, then?"

"No, thank you," replied Ella. "I don't think we'll be drinking cups of tea again for some little while."

"This is not a formal interview..." began the policeman.

"Oh, yes, it is," interrupted Frank. "Turn the recorder on, please."

"Okay, sir. If you insist."

"I do."

"Right. This interview is being conducted by Police Sergeant Cornworthy and Police Constable Tigley. For the benefit of the tape please tell us your names."

"My name is Ella Raleigh."

"My name is Frank Raleigh, her husband."

"Thank you. Please tell us how you came to be on the Buckfastleigh to Totnes train?"

"We went to meet Dudley Weston after his wife came to tell us that he'd run away. We were helping the East Devon Police to investigate the suspected murder of Anthony Buckerell, a Budleigh Salterton solicitor." Frank paused for breath.

Ella took over. "Dudley Weston phoned us and lured us to his cottage. We thought we were helping him. He gave us drugged cups of tea, tied us up and tried to get us to confess to this murder. He seemed to think that because Frank was in the room with Anthony Buckerell when he died that Frank must have done it."

"He didn't seem to understand that I was in the presence of a police officer all the time. Both the police and ourselves think the murder was impossible."

"And anyway, we're not likely to be trying to solve a murder that we committed, are we?"

"Right, if I may interrupt you for a second. You seem to have answered most of the questions I was planning to ask but not the question I asked."

"We escaped from the cottage, ran through the woods and stumbled onto the railway line right in front of the train. It was going so slowly it stopped without running us over. They let us get on board and took us to Totnes where you arrested us!"

The female officer leaned forward and asked Ella. "What's the name of the police officer who was in the room when the murder supposedly took place?"

"WPC Elsie Knowle. A wonderful police officer who will, one day, make a fine detective."

The door opened and another police officer walked in. "I heard that. That's very kind of you to say that, Ella!"

"WPC Knowle has entered the room."

"I heard about your little escapade. May I sit down?"

The policeman quickly scurried to bring in another chair.

"May we turn the recorder off, now?" WPC Knowle asked.

Frank nodded. The policewoman, Sergeant Cornworthy, nodded and the policeman, PC Tigley, pressed a switch to halt the recording.

"I thought you promised to let me know when you went gallivanting about the countryside?"

"We tried to phone you. We left a message."

"Yes, I heard it. Do you know how many pubs have bus shelters outside them?"

"No?"

"You forgot to tell me the name of the village! A fine detective you'll make!"

"Sorry. Stupid mistake."

"Luckily Lizzie here sent out a message to us in East Devon when Dudley came to see her. I saw your names and thought

I'd come down to see what was going on."

"Dudley Weston came into the police station?"

"Yes," Lizzie Cornworthy replied, "he told us the story about Frank Raleigh being the only one who could have killed Anthony Buckerell. He convinced me and my colleague to take the matter further. PC Tigley suggested we arrest at the railway station to stop you running away."

"How did you know we were on the train?"

"You were followed by Dudley Weston. He phoned me to tell me how you'd stopped the train."

"I thought there was someone with us in those woods!" groaned Ella.

"Right, let's clear up the formalities." WPC Knowle turned to her colleagues. "There's no way either Mr. or Mrs. Raleigh could have murdered Mr. Buckerell. The toxicology report came in today and it makes very interesting reading."

"OK, WPC Knowle." Sergeant Cornworthy looked at Frank and Ella. "We will not be taking this matter any further. You are free to go."

"Oh no, they are not free to go." WPC Knowle retorted. "We need to have a brainstorming session and we're going to use this room. Lizzie, can your colleague rustle up any tea?"

"No tea, please. We'll both have coffee."

WPC Knowle explained what conclusion the report had reached. "It seems he died from the administering of a poison called Thamacin."

"But how? We were both there."

"True. However, he wasn't poisoned in the cell. He was poisoned two days earlier. Let me read you the history of Thamacin and you'll understand."

She got out a piece of paper from her pocket and began to read.

"Thamacin is extracted from a plant with a Latin name of Cleistanthus nux-vomica commonly called Ottan Ettinareem. The plant and its poison is only found in South East Asia. Europeans first discovered it when a Jesuit priest called Father Amuccin was travelling in Siam in South East Asia in the early twentieth century. It was originally intended to be used as a natural herbal bodybuilder. It was meant to build up muscle fat. It was also used to promote good health when the body was poisoned.

Father Amuccin, the discoverer of the poison, took it to prove it had no ill effects. The tribes where the plant grows know that it has to be boiled in spring water for three days to bleed all the poison out of it. Father Amuccin only boiled it for two. Nobody mentioned that to Father Amuccin. Two days after drinking it, he died.

A small tablet of Thamacin kills exactly two days after digestion by means of clogging up the arteries to the heart and causing a heart attack."

"Exactly two days?" Ella asked.

"Yes, strange but true."

"So, when our murderer sent the message about dying..."

Frank quoted the seventeen words as if they were etched on his heart. "You will die in the seventh hour of the night on the seventh day of the year."

"Dudley, our murderer, must have known about this time-lapse and poisoned the solicitor exactly two days previously," WPC Knowle concluded.

"Dudley Weston?" asked the policewoman called Lizzie.

"Maybe. However, we've discovered four Dudleys who each had a grievance against Anthony Buckerell."

"And," Frank added, "who were each being blackmailed by

the solicitor."

"Well, at least, three of them were," interrupted Ella. "We haven't spoken to the last Dudley yet."

"That's going to be our next interview, I think."

"Are you sure you don't want police support? I could ask PC Hydon to go with you."

"No," said Ella quickly, "he may frighten the final Dudley from talking. PC Hydon can be quite intimidating sometimes."

"What about the Doctor?" asked WPC Knowle.

"He's not called Dudley. And he was in Thailand on holiday. You checked with Heathrow."

"Yes, I wasn't happy with that," mused WPC Knowle. "Don't disregard him. You may want to interview him as well. Just to be on the safe side."

"It's interesting that so far our suspects all have an enthusiasm for exotic plants!" Ella voiced the thought that Frank had been considering.

"South East Asia, you said. The poison came from there?"

"I wonder if it's found anywhere else in the world?"

"It didn't say so. But it's worth checking."

"Right," said WPC Knowle, "a plan of action is coming together. You will both carefully and politely interview both the last Dudley and the good doctor. Don't upset them or scare them. There's a good chance they're innocent! I've got to get back to East Devon. We're so busy at the moment."

"Thank you for coming down here to help us out," said Ella.

"Not a problem. How are you getting back to Otterbury?"

"Our car should still be at Staverton Station. Can we scrounge a lift back to the car?"

PC Tigley coughed and ventured, "I think we can help there. Show us where Dudley Weston is living now. I want to have a word with him. For my own peace of mind. You stay in the car and I'll drop you at Staverton after my quick word."

Sergeant Cornworthy nodded her approval.

They soon found their way to Staverton and with the help of a large-scale Ordnance Survey map, they managed to find the cottage at the end of a long muddy track. It was locked and deserted. There was no answer despite loud hammerings on the doors and windows by PC Tigley. Frank and Ella were not surprised.

They made their way back to their car parked under the trees on the road by Staverton Station.

As they reached the level crossing, they saw a figure crouched by the car.

"That's Dudley Weston!"

PC Tigley brought the car to a screeching halt. Dudley turned towards them.

"Police! Police! Here's the escaped criminal's car. I've found it!"

PC Tigley, Frank and Ella got out of the car.

"You've caught them already!"

"Dudley, what were you doing?"

Dudley ignored the question.

"Officer, they're out to get me. They've killed once. Don't let them kill again."

"Sir," shouted PC Tigley. "Stand still. I want a word with you!"

"No chance. Not with them around."

Dudley Weston turned away and ran down the road. PC Tigley gave chase. Dudley dodged into the woods surrounding the road hoping to evade capture but there was no evading PC Tigley. He was a very fit and proficient athlete. In no time at all, PC Tigley had brought Dudley down with a stylish rugby tackle. Frank and Ella ambled behind but were close enough to see and hear Dudley's cries.

"Get off. It's not me you should be chasing."

PC Tigley lifted Dudley to his feet whilst keeping a firm hand on his collar.

"It's those two back at the car."

Dudley wriggled and squirmed but was unable to escape.

"They've probably halfway to Exeter by now!"

"Actually, we're not. We're standing right behind you."

Frank and Ella stood there looking down on him. "You caught them? Well done. They won't dare run away from you!"

"Be quiet, sir!" commanded PC Tigley.

Dudley was guided, by PC Tigley, back down the path from which he'd been chased. Frank and Ella followed behind.

As they walked, PC Tigley informed Dudley that he, PC Tigley, knew, for certain, that Frank and Ella Raleigh did not commit the murder. They had a cast-iron alibi. They had not even met Anthony Buckerell until the day before he died.

Frank noticed that PC Tigley did not add that Frank had not met Anthony until the day after he was poisoned!

"I am completely satisfied that those two are innocent."

"Hmpph!"

"Unlike your good self, Mr. Weston. You appear to be trying to desperately shift suspicion away from you. Are you hiding something?"

"Me? I've told my story to these two. I told them the truth."

"Have you ever travelled to South East Asia?"

"No, don't be silly. I've never even been out of this country."

"What about your exotic plants? Are they from South East Asia?"

"No. They're from New Zealand. And most of them are not exotic. I collect ferns that are native to New Zealand. My piece de resistance is *Myosotis traversii*. It's thought to be extinct. I may have the only one of its species outside of the Orokana Ecosanctuary. It's not poisonous. It's a harmless rare fern."

"And what about your kidnapping?"

"What do you mean?"

"You kidnapped Mr. and Mrs. Raleigh. You held them against their will."

"I thought they were murderers. I'm still not one hundred per cent convinced."

"Well, sir. I'd like to hear more about your reasons for keeping Mr. and Mrs. Raleigh captive. And I'd be happy to provide you with further proof concerning Mr. and Mrs. Raleigh's innocence. So, either I arrest you or you can volunteer to accompany me to the police station in Totnes?"

"I'll come quietly. I don't have much choice, do I?"

"No, sir. You don't."

Back at Staverton Station, Frank and Ella checked their car but could find no evidence of any damage. The car started the first time, as usual. PC Tigley took a quick but thorough look under the bonnet and suggested they drive carefully back to their home. Frank and Ella both thanked him for his help.

PC Tigley and Dudley Weston got into the police car and drove away to Totnes.

When they reached home, they showered, changed clothes, had a hearty meal and settled down to some escapism on the television.

The next afternoon Frank informed Ella. "I'm just going to phone Mrs. Weston. Ask her if she's alright," said Frank.

"Is that wise?"

"I've lost any sympathy that I ever had for Dudley Weston. He deserves an angry wife!"

As Frank expected, the phone was answered by Mrs. Weston. He turned the phone to loudspeaker mode so that Ella could hear both ends of the conversation.

"Thank you for phoning. Yes, he arrived home today just in time for his dinner. I made him his favourite. He's so pleased to be home. And I'm so pleased to have him home. I do love him!"

"Tell him we're glad to be of help."

"Thank you, I will. Goodbye."

Frank put the phone down. Frank and Ella looked at each other. No words were necessary.

CHAPTER 13
THE INSURANCE COMPANY PAYOUT

"Dudley Musbury," announced Ella. "His address is here on the copy of his letter of complaint."

Yesterday's escape and arrest seemed a lifetime away. Both Ella and Frank wanted to complete the interviews so that they could gather all the evidence together and start to formulate some answers to the questions surrounding Anthony Buckerell's murder.

So, they set off for the Musbury residence located in one of the roads leading off Greenway Lane in a quiet residential area of Budleigh Salterton.

They decided not to phone ahead and just hoped that Dudley was in.

Frank theorised. "Don't give him time to prepare himself and we may get more of the truth."

Dudley's house was a modest Edwardian terrace stacked alongside many others in one of a number of cul-de-sacs. A brick wall topped with railings separated this cul-de-sac from a modern, sterile housing estate. It caused a startling clash between two distinct architectural styles.

Ella looked at the difference. "I think I prefer the older

buildings. They seem to be more Devonian somehow. Those modern houses could be located anywhere in the British Isles."

"I take your point. I guess there are replicas of those same houses in many an edge of town estate."

"Phone App working?"

"Yes, all switched on!"

"Fully charged?"

"Of course!"

They rang the bell and around-shouldered man about Ella's height answered the door. Ella recognised him from the funeral. She could also see that, recently, he had been crying.

"Yes, can I help you?" His voice was quiet and morose.

"I certainly hope so." Frank smiled. "We're helping Anthony Buckerell's secretary to sort out a few loose ends concerning his will."

"Now's not a good time."

"We won't take up too much of it, then. We need to ask you some questions about his will."

"So how does that affect me?"

"Well, we don't know yet. That's why we're here!"

"Well, as long as you're quick, I suppose, you'd better come in. Please keep the noise down. My wife is asleep upstairs, and I don't want her disturbed." He sniffed into a tissue before throwing it away into a small, overflowing wastepaper bin perched beneath the telephone table in the hallway.

They went into the back room and Dudley Musbury invited them to sit down at the table. Ella noticed that the wooden chairs were reminiscent of the ones in Dudley Weston's cottage at Staverton.

"How can I help?" He continued to speak in a quiet, monotoned voice.

Ella smiled in a friendly manner and began. "Mrs. Aylesbeare, Mr. Buckerell's secretary, showed us a letter of complaint that you wrote to him. I was interested in why you wrote it?"

Dudley put his hands together as if playing a game of cat's cradle. He looked at neither Frank nor Ella as he answered the question.

"That's an easy question to answer. I'd written that letter in ninety-nine different ways over the years and never sent it. The hundredth time I plucked up enough courage to send it. I wanted something on the record."

"Why?"

"We had a meeting in his office a couple of months ago."

"Sit down, Mr. Musbury."

He had such a smarmy smile when he knew you couldn't touch him. Condescending little oik!

"I haven't got much time. I'm due at the theatre in about half an hour. Rehearsals. I've got a small part in the new production."

"Yes, we all know. I'm not needed until later this month."

"Behind the scenes staff never are. Now, how's your lovely wife?"

"She'll never be the same!"

"Well, at least, you've got the insurance payout. Thanks to me."

"What's left of it. There's wasn't much once you'd taken your slice."

"Excuse me, I did a lot of work on your behalf. And don't forget that certain facts that the police never quite learned about it…."

"That's why I'm here!"

"Certain facts would have caused you to receive no payments whatsoever."

"But enough is enough. Most solicitors charge a set fee. It's a once-only payment. You've taken your fee every year."

"Well, if you're not happy, you could always go to another solicitor. I'd be most willing to pass on your information - all your information - to your new solicitor. And, of course, to the police."

"That's blackmail!"

"No, it's not. I'm doing it for your own protection. Your wife's protection. For both of your continual protection. That's why I charge a fee each year."

"You know, Mr. Buckerell, one of these days…"

"I hope you're not intending to threaten me. Let me remind you. On that night you were driving the car. You were too busy talking lovey-dovey to your wife instead of concentrating on the road."

"You don't need to remind me."

"It was your fault you left the road. It was your fault you hit the tree. It was your fault that your wife is in a wheelchair."

"Yes, I'm well aware of that."

"You and only you are to blame! Not the wet road. Not the phantom other driver that nobody managed to track down. You!"

"Yes, I know!"

"And I have made sure that the funding for your wife's health-care comes through each month. I make sure your insurance company pays you that regular amount. Even though, if all the facts were known, they should not be paying out. Should they?"

"No, but…"

"There's are no buts. You are a very lucky man to have me around to help you. A very lucky man!"

"To have a maimed wife? To have nightmares most nights? To

be unable to work and provide for my darling wife? Very lucky indeed!! I ought to run you over and see how you feel!"

"Now, that would be a very silly idea. I keep meticulous records of all my clients. The police would soon find out about you. Now. I don't want to be late for my rehearsal. I have a part to prepare for in our new production. This meeting is over."

Dudley Musbury sat there, hands still cradled, tears rolling down his sad, colourless face. The effort of recalling the meeting with the solicitor was almost overwhelming.

Ella passed him a tissue from her handbag.

"Thank you, Mr. Musbury. That must have been a difficult story to tell?"

"No, it's good to get it off my chest. It doesn't matter now anyway."

"Now that Mr. Buckerell's dead and buried? But your confession...?"

"My confession? That's what doesn't matter."

"Why, I'm afraid I don't follow?"

"It's my wife. Her life has been worse than useless this last year. On top of the injuries from the accident, she's been diagnosed with severe rheumatoid arthritis. It's like she's dying. Slowly dying. She's been begging me to give her an overdose for the last few weeks. And so, just before you rang the bell, I did!"

CHAPTER 14
YOU'RE SITTING OPPOSITE THE STAR

Frank immediately phoned for an ambulance and quickly explained the situation. Ella, meanwhile, contacted the police. Dudley Musbury just sat there at the table with his hands still cradled staring at the patterned wallpaper.

They arrived together. Two paramedics in green coveralls raced upstairs. PC Hydon followed them to check on the state of Dudley's wife whilst WPC Knowle went into the back room and sat down next to Dudley. They conversed in silence.

A couple of minutes later, Mrs. Musbury was carried gently in the arms of PC Hydon down the stairs and out into the ambulance. There were gasps from a couple of neighbours standing outside on the pavement. The paramedics quickly made Mrs. Musbury comfortable in the back of the ambulance. One stayed with her and the other climbed into the driver's seat. Ten seconds later the ambulance drove off. PC Hydon stood there on the pavement listening to its siren becoming fainter and fainter as the vehicle sped along the Newton Poppleford road towards Exeter.

He turned towards the gaggle of gawping neighbours and, in a firm voice, uttered the well-worn cliche.

"Move along, there. Nothing left to see here. Haven't you got homes to go to?"

The gaggle sighed and dispersed.

PC Hydon rubbed his chin and ambled back into the house to find Ella standing on her own in the hallway.

"Where's Frank?"

"In the kitchen making mugs of tea."

"Excellent idea." He called towards the kitchen. "Three sugars for me!"

Ella stood there, feeling redundant, not knowing what she should do.

"It's like a tomb in here," remarked PC Hydon.

"For a policeman, that was most un-PC!" Ella snapped. Then, considering her reply, she grinned, "Must tell Frank that one!"

"I heard it!" Frank came out of the kitchen carrying a tray laden with mugs and biscuits. "Sugar's on the worktop by the sink, PC Hydon! Teaspoons in the drawer by the cooker."

Frank deposited the tray on the table and turned back towards the door to leave WPC Knowle and Dudley to their silence.

"Don't go," said Dudley in a quiet voice.

"OK," replied Frank.

"I've got something to say, and I want you to hear it as well."

Frank sat down on one of the two vacant chairs at the table.

"Anthony Buckerell was blackmailing me. So, I killed him."

"Pardon?" said WPC Knowle.

"It's true, I killed him. Take me away. I don't want to be here anymore."

"Are you telling me, you killed Anthony Buckerell at Otterbury Police Station?"

"Yes, wherever it was. I killed him. Where do you take your

murderers? Can we go there?

"Right, if you say so. Dudley Musbury, I'm arresting you for the murder of Anthony Buckerell."

And for the second time in recent days Frank heard a police officer recite "Sir, you do not have to say anything. But it may harm your defence if you do not mention when questioned something which you later rely on in Court. Anything you do say may be given in evidence."

"I understand. Let's go."

PC Hydon had heard all that had been said. He came in and helped Dudley Musbury up and shepherded him out to their police car.

WPC Knowle quickly closed all windows and doors and ushered Frank and Ella out of the house.

"That was horrible," sighed Ella as they drove home to Otterbury. "I feel so sorry for both of them. I find it hard to believe he's our murderer."

"Even though he might have just killed his wife?"

"That's a dreadful thing to say."

"I know, but this is a dreadful business. We're mixing with some desperate people and, at least one of them is probably a murderer!"

"You're right, but sometimes, I find what we're doing to be so difficult..."

"Well, we may just have handed it all over to the police. If he's our murderer then our job is done."

That night Ella said a quick but earnest prayer for Mrs. Musbury. It must have been heard because the next morning,

WPC Knowle phoned to say that Mrs. Musbury was alive.

"Very weak and fragile, but alive."

"That's great news," enthused Frank. "What about Dudley?"

"Dudley Musbury is still in our custody. The detectives at Exeter are interviewing him. I sat in on the first interview and he's talking a load of rubbish. So far, he's told us three different ways in which he killed Anthony Buckerell. He even told us about a blowpipe with which he fired a poisonous dart. When someone asked him how he'd fired it through the walls of the cell, he said it was a drone that flew down the chimney. I remarked that there was no chimney in the room. Then he said he shot him with a high-velocity rifle from a room overlooking Exeter police station."

"But Anthony Buckerell died in Otterbury?"

"Exactly. They're going to release him as long as he stays in the area. I'll make sure that Mental Health in Exeter takes up his case."

When Frank explained about the overdose Dudley said he gave his wife, WPC Knowle sighed. "Well, she's not dead yet. We'll cross that bridge if anything horrific comes of it."

"Where will he stay? He can't go home, can he?"

"No, he'll be going to stay with another Dudley for a few days. When he's not visiting the hospital, that is."

"Another Dudley?"

"He mentioned some of his friends to us. We rang around and talked to Dudley Widworthy. They seem to be friends. He told us that they met at the local amateur dramatic society. They're both members. Widworthy's an actor and Musbury the stage manager."

"I wonder if all four Dudleys are in the same society?"

"It wouldn't surprise me. You'll need to check it out! Have you been to see the good doctor yet?"

"No. Ella's on to that. She's booked an appointment for

tomorrow."

"Is Budleigh Salterton your local surgery?"

"Yes, there's no surgery in Otterbury so it's either here or Sidmouth. When we first arrived, we chose Budleigh because the name sounded nicer!"

"Perfectly sound reason to choose a medical practice!"

"We've been in East Devon all these years and this is only about the third time we've had to go."

"What's her reason for her appointment?"

"She's suffering from a lack of well-being, whatever that means? Still, it gets you an appointment with the doctor!"

The doctor's surgery in Budleigh Salterton was crowded but Ella arrived armed with her Kindle and was prepared to wait patiently. Eventually, her name was called, and she found herself sitting opposite Doctor Moore.

"Good morning and how are you feeling?"

"A bit down."

"Ella Raleigh, isn't it? I've got your records up on the screen. You're healthy. We've hardly ever seen you here. I'm bamboozled. My colleague normally deals with the out-of-town patients."

"You were recommended by Mrs. Aylesbeare, Anthony Buckerell's secretary."

"Anthony's dead, isn't he?"

"Yes, it's so sad."

"Yes, I heard about it when I arrived back from Thailand."

"Well, that's the reason I wanted to talk to you, Doctor."

"I don't understand?"

"You knew him, didn't you? You treated him for a number of

years."

"I did, on a regular basis. Yes."

The Doctor sat there contemplating.

"Wait a minute. Did you come here because you're depressed or is there an ulterior motive?"

"I'm sorry, Doctor. You see my husband and I are helping Mrs. Aylesbeare sort out Mr. Buckerell's affairs and there are questions that need answering."

"I don't think this is the time or place for an interrogation, Mrs. Raleigh."

"Well, I..."

"You're not ill, are you? Befogged, maybe, but not ill?"

"Not really, no."

"Look, meet me this evening at the Otter Inn in Colaton Raleigh. It's quiet and we can talk."

"No."

"Sorry?"

"No, I won't meet you there. My husband and I will. He thinks you know something about Mr. Buckerell's death. He says you could be most helpful especially with the reading of the will at the end of the week. Otherwise, people might think you were taking me out on a date."

"I never meant..."

"And I wouldn't want to sully the reputation of a well-respected local doctor!"

"That visit to Doctor Moore did my well-being a power of good!"

"Excellent, I didn't even know your well-being was ill."

"He tried to ask me out for a meal!"

"Excellent, you could have pumped him for information."

"Frank Raleigh, are you listening to a word I'm saying?"

"Yes, of course. We've been married long enough for me to trust you totally."

"Thank you. But I'm not sure I trust the good Doctor to behave himself."

"If he lays one finger on you, I'll knock his block off!"

"He won't."

"Why not?"

"Because you'll be there as well!"

"Charge up your phone!"

The Otter Inn was quiet. The food was excellent and both Frank and Ella vowed to return there as a couple in the near future. The conversation was stilted at first. However, Doctor Moore had a glass of wine and was soon breaching some code of confidentiality.

"I heard he was poisoned by the police. Probably the food!"

Frank looked around at the half-empty room. No-one was near enough to be able to listen in on their conversation.

"No, he wasn't poisoned by the police," replied Frank.

"He was poisoned, and the police have identified at least four suspects." Ella carefully told the doctor some of the salient facts about the case - the letters and the blackmail.

"Four Dudleys? I know them all. They're all members of the local amateur dramatic society, the Budleigh Players. My word, you've got a tough task there."

"Why?"

"Well, as I told that lovely young lady police officer the other day, they're all pretty suspicious people. I could easily imagine any one of them could be your murderer."

"Really, even Dudley Musbury?"

"Especially Dudley Musbury. Ever since his wife was maimed in that sad accident, Dudley's behaviour has been excessive. They say he becomes very violent. I haven't treated him for it, but I have heard."

"What?"

"No, I've said too much. He's normally such a pleasant, quiet character. Works wonders behind the scenes. Although saying that, he has to be the untidiest stage manager I've ever worked with in all my acting career."

"What about Dudley Gosford-Feniton? He writes plays, doesn't he?"

"The professor? No, just pantomimes. However, I've never seen Anthony in one of his pantomimes. Well, never in an important role. Back in the chorus or the back of the horse!"

"Why is that?"

"Well, the word is that Dudley lost out on some inheritance. People thought Anthony was to blame. I can't imagine the Professor killing. Although you said it was poisoning. With all his tropical plants - we share a passion for the exotic in botany - he might know something about poisons. It's all way beyond me!"

Doctor Moore took another swig of wine.

"Now, Dudley Weston. I have treated him. And without giving too much away, he's sick - lovesick. Mr. Buckerell bamboozled Mr. Weston's sweetheart into marrying him and not Dudley. As you can imagine, Dudley was not a happy man. You don't think he could have killed him because of that, do you? No!"

Ella's phone was lying in her lap recording every word.

"Well, who does that leave us with?" Doctor Moore looked around him as he wracked his brain for the last Dudley.

"Oh, I know. Dudley Widworthy. Now he was, and probably

still is, his own worst enemy. He was a terrible businessman. If I was befogged enough to want to lose ten thousand pounds, I would give it to him. He'd lose it in a week!"

"We heard that he had a business selling herbal medicine. Did he contact you?"

"I saw straight away the business was doomed. He was soon bankrupt. Now you come to mention it, didn't he blame Anthony Buckerell for his failure?"

"Did he?"

"Yes, I think so. Well, that was stupid. He had only himself to blame. I wouldn't have touched his herbal business with a barge pole!"

"What about you, Doctor Moore? Did Anthony Buckerell ever cause you any problems?"

"Like what?"

"Like Blackmail?"

"Blackmail? Don't be so silly. I'm not a businessman. The surgery is run by a very efficient business manager. I play no part in the finances. He didn't nab my wife. I'm single. And I've never had the opportunity to inherit any money. I live a quiet life. My work, my plants and my drama."

"No other problems?"

"No, apart from the licence. But that was sorted."

"I don't understand?"

"The theatrical licence for my latest starring role. I heard on the grapevine that Anthony was amongst a dwindling few who were opposing the licence. Probably on the grounds that the noise and congestion on opening night would bring Budleigh Salterton to a standstill." He laughed. "So, so absurd."

Daniel finished off his wine and sat back with a contented look upon his face.

"Yes, we had some problems. At one point recently it was cancelled. But we persevered and nothing came of it. Anthony died before the committee could meet. The show will go on."

Frank looked around at the room which had almost emptied since the start of their meal. Even the waitress was nowhere in sight.

"When did you last see Anthony Buckerell alive?"

"Well, I've been on holiday for the last while or so. I suppose I must have seen him just before Christmas, maybe late December. Sometime before he died, I guess."

"Didn't you meet up with him each month to give him a vitamin supplement?"

"Yes, who told you that? He didn't like pills and tablets but would willingly let me inject him each month."

"When was the last time you injected him?" Ella asked.

"I used to inject him at the beginning of each month. Mind you, the Dudleys you all mentioned did meet up with him at around the same time. Maybe, even a little later than I did. They attended a meeting about the licensing issue. I was unable to go, I was just about to leave for my holiday. But I'm pretty sure that the four met up with him to discuss the problem."

The waitress had appeared from the bar area, so Frank asked her for the bill.

"No, let me pay for all of us. I'm in a celebratory mood. You're sitting opposite the star of Table for Four, the Budleigh Players' biggest ever production at the Public Halls. With that licence approval last week, nothing is going to prevent the world from discovering that Daniel Moore was born to be a star.

"Well done!"

"Thank you. This time next year, I will be on the stage in the West End!"

Frank and Ella arrived home in Otterbury at just after half-past ten. They had just settled down to a cup of late-night tea when the phone rang.

"Bit late for a phone call," said Frank.

As he about to pick up the receiver, Ella hissed. "Activate the recorder."

"Good idea."

He did and then picked up the phone. "Hello, good evening. How can I help you?"

"You're way beyond that! You can't help anyone, can you? You're just plain stupid."

"You again! What do you want?"

The voice was again a little muffled and obviously disguised. It still wasn't possible to tell if it was male or female.

"Still calling yourself detectives? You interview people and you never ask the right questions."

"Thank you for your opinion but who am I listening to?"

"It doesn't matter who I am. I'm not the failure. Dudley told me all about your efforts. You're no stars. You're the laughing stock of East Devon. Baffled? Befogged? Bested? Befuddled? Bamboozled? Beleaguered? The list goes on!"

"Are you drunk?"

"Only on the sweet taste of my impending, my continuing success. I've said too much!"

The connection was immediately broken.

"That was our killer again. I wonder if he's made his first mistake. If so, then I think we've got him!"

CHAPTER 15
WHERE THERE'S A WILL, THERE'S A WAY

The next morning Alice Aylesbeare phoned and asked to speak to Ella.

"The reading of the will is this afternoon at three o'clock. I'd like to invite you two along. Mr. Buckerell didn't leave anything to you, of course, but I thought you'd find it interesting."

"That's very kind of you. Who else is going to be there?"

"The four Dudleys, the good doctor, a solicitor from Sidmouth to make sure I do everything correctly and your two police friends. Just, in case..."

"You mean, in case it gets out of hand?"

"No, we're very civilised in Budleigh Salterton."

"Of course, we'll be there. Three o'clock at the late Mr. Buckerell's office?"

"Indeed!"

"Do you need any help beforehand?"

"Well, I've made some cupcakes and I'm bringing tea and coffee."

"Frank and I will be happy to play the part of waiter and waitress."

"That would be most efficacious."

Ella explained to Frank about the plans for the afternoon. They decided to start the day with a short walk from Budleigh Salterton followed by a leisurely lunch before heading for the solicitor's office in time to help to dispense the refreshments.

The weather was decidedly pleasant for the time of year, so they donned suitable clothing, put their walking boots in the car and set off via Newton Poppleford for Budleigh. They'd discovered a little car park in Brook Road behind the High Street. They parked there for free and headed into the High Street. They crossed straight over and walked up Cliff Road towards the sea. They joined the South West Coast Path but unlike the other week, they were not headed for West Down Beacon, but eastwards towards the mouth of the River Otter.

Ella had been reading about the derivation of Budleigh Salterton's name: "The Abbot of Otterton Priory employed thirty-three salters who made a living out of salt panning."

"Hence the Salter's Town?"

"Yes. However, the parish of Budleigh Salterton only came into being during the last decade of the nineteenth century."

"It's quite the new town."

"Even though salting may go back to Roman times."

"You're a regular hive of knowledge."

"Yes, and I'm not even using my phone."

"I'm never going to live that down, am I?"

"Certainly not!"

They wandered along the promenade. The beach huts had been put away for the winter although the cafe was still open.

Frank eyes twinkled as he took out his phone. "I, for my part, did find one excerpt from an article in the May 1937 Express and Echo that made me laugh."

"Go on, then. Read it!"

"The anonymous author wrote 'In these days when noise has all but swept the entire land like a tidal wave, such places as Budleigh Salterton are like the green oases which dot the desert. Here the tired traveller may rest awhile in the sure knowledge that body and mind will be refreshed.'"

Ella laughed loudly.

"Well, the recent events have disproved that article straightaway!" roared Frank.

"I think we can say that unfortunately, times have changed!"

A passing pedestrian gave them a strange disbelieving look. Frank and Ella were struck by a wave of embarrassment and hurried on silently towards the Lime Kiln carpark.

Frank knew the history of this name. "There's an old lime kiln at the car park entrance."

Reaching the carpark, the lime kiln stood in the middle of the road playing a new role as a traffic island. A blue plaque described its original usage.

They continued on the promenade as it made a direct path towards the mouth of the River Otter. Ella quietly took out a piece of paper from her pocket without Frank observing her.

"The beach is composed of cobble sand pebbles known as the Bunter Pebble Beds."

"They weren't named after Billy Bunter?"

"No!"

"Or Lord Peter Wimsey's Bunter?"

"No! As you probably already know, they were named after the German Buntsandstein."

"Bunt - Sand - Stein?"

"Yes, meaning variegated or colourful. You see, I can show off too!"

"A giant river that geologists have named Budleighensis used to flow across this landscape about 240 million years ago. "

"Budleigh - en -sis?"

"Good pronunciation!"

"A bit before our time."

Ella surreptitiously placed the scrap of paper back in her pocket.

"The pebbles and sand were deposited all around this area. They dried out and were then compressed into those red cliffs."

"Those trees look like they've been there forever."

"They're Scots pines and they're not that old! Less than a century, some say."

Frank thought it was time to join in with the information sharing.

"Did you know that a local painter and decorator was fined by East Devon District Council for taking away a bucket full of pebbles from the beach?"

"Why?"

"He broke a local bye-law from the 1949 Coastal Protection Act."

"I seem to remember reading about that. Didn't the mayor blame TV gardening programmes for suggesting using rocks in water features."

Frank and Ella enjoyed the bantering exchange of trivial information. It always enhanced their walks and made the surroundings come alive!

They returned to the car park and made their way inland and across it to continue on the Coast Path. The lowest bridge to cross the River Otter was a little way upstream. On their right were the salt marshes. They stopped at a bird hide and using the helpful information on display managed to spot a little egret, a small white heron.

They soon reached the bridge and stood on it for a while, enjoying the quiet solitude all around them. In front of them, the river rolled on to the river mouth. Behind them lay a walk they had enjoyed many times before. Up to Otterton and on to Colaton Raleigh.

"Times getting on," said Frank. "Let's cut off part of the walk to the aqueduct and head along the road."

They headed westwards along South Farm Road. Before they reached the corner that led up to the main road, they turned seawards and back to the carpark.

"Just a short walk today," said Ella.

"But enough to work up an appetite."

They strolled back along the promenade into Budleigh Salterton and found what was fast becoming one of their favourite eateries near the garage. An hour and an half drifted by in a haze of food, drink and pleasant conversation.

"Time for the will!" Ella paid the bill and they sauntered hand in hand up the High Street to the solicitor's office.

They arrived before any of the others and helped Mrs. Aylesbeare with the chairs. They set out the drinks and cakes on a mahogany table and then sat and watched the old grandfather clock that stood proudly in the corner, as its hands moved slowly towards three o'clock.

One by one the tramping of feet on the wooden stairs announced the arrival of the invitees. Mrs. Aylesbeare stood by the door and welcomed each arrival. Ella offered them tea or coffee and Frank passed around a well-stocked plate of biscuits and cupcakes.

PC Hydon and WPC Knowle arrived last of all. They apologised for their lateness and promised to sit quietly in the corner unless called upon.

Mrs. Aylesbeare went and sat herself comfortably in Anthony

Buckerell's old leather chair behind his old leather-covered mahogany desk. She had a clutch of papers in front of her and a smart embossed file in her hands.

"Good afternoon, everyone. Thank you for attending. I won't delay any further, other than asking you to refrain from asking questions or making comments until I have finished reading the will. Is that acceptable to us all?"

Everyone nodded their heads in agreement.

"Excellent. If we're sitting comfortably, then I'll begin."

She opened the embossed file and took out a sheet of paper.

"I, Anthony Algernon Buckerell, of The Haven, Budleigh Salterton, revoke all former testamentary dispositions made by me and declare this to be my last will.

I appoint Alice Marigold Aylesbeare, my loyal and long-suffering office secretary, to be the sole executor of this will. Should she be unable to fulfil this function then I appoint Daniel Aldous Huxley Dudley Moore to be my sole executor.

I make provision the following legacies to be left to the following specific beneficiaries.

Firstly, the sum of Five Thousand Pounds to Alice Marigold Aylesbeare my loyal and long-suffering office secretary.

Secondly, I ask for my executor to buy one National Lottery ticket for every person in the parish of Budleigh Salterton whose name appears on the Electoral Roll.

Then special gifts to the following beneficiaries.

The sum of ten thousand, one hundred and fifty-two pounds to Dudley Arnold Syon Gosford-Feniton in the calculation of payments made.

The sum of twelve thousand, four hundred pounds to Dudley Steven Weston in the calculation of payments made.

The sum of eight thousand pounds to Dudley Musbury in the calculation of fees claimed.

The sum of twenty-four thousand, nine hundred and ninety-nine pounds to Dudley William Widworthy in respect of the purchase of stock made by me during these last years. The only proviso to this legacy is that the money must be invested in an income draw-down account. The beneficiary will forfeit all of the money if the money is used in any way in investing in any business.

The residuary estate to the maximum amount of five thousand pounds to Daniel Aldous Huxley Dudley Moore. The only proviso to this legacy is that he immediately leaves the Budleigh Players and takes no acting part in any production of said company for the next ten years.

After all these bequests and conditions are met, then the final residuary estate will be placed in the Buckerell Trust.

The Buckerell Trust will be set up to ensure that this office and its contents will be used for the sole profession of a town solicitor. The person appointed must remain in the post for a minimum of ten years. The post of office secretary will be open to the employment of Alice Marigold Aylesbeare for as long as she so wishes.

In Witness whereof, I have here unto set my hand this thirteenth day of September 2015.

Signed by the above-named testator Anthony Algernon Buckerell as his last will in the presence of us both present at the same time who at his request and in his presence and in the presence of each other have signed our names below as witnesses. Elspeth Trill and Arthur Hogchester."

The room was silent. Mrs. Aylesbeare returned the sheet of paper into the embossed file and turned towards WPC

Knowle.

"That's it. Mr. Buckerell left me five thousand pounds in the will. Am I allowed to benefit from the will if I'm an executor?"

"I'm sure you must be."

Frank chipped in from the back of the room. "Well, there was one very strange bequest. He asked you to buy a lottery ticket for everyone on the electoral roll in Budleigh Salterton!"

WPC Knowle laughed: "How extraordinary! I've never heard of that before."

"No, I hadn't either. He also asked me in his will to find someone to take over the solicitors. He would give the whole practice to them if they promised to stay in Budleigh Salterton for ten years. Oh, and they had to employ me as well!"

"That was generous." Dudley Weston had finally found his voice.

Ella disagreed. "Not so much generous, as essential. No-one could take over this office and not rely upon Alice's expertise."

Mrs. Aylesbeare blushed. She did not intend to become the centre of attention. "Any other comments or questions?"

Professor Gosford-Feniton smiled. "Yes, this is all most unlike him. He wasn't the philanthropic sort. As you can see, he didn't spend that much on decoration or modern equipment. If it was good enough for Dickens, it was good enough for him!"

Ella looked around her and spoke to Alice. "You could change that. Update the place. It would make it more appealing to his successor."

"Yes, maybe. There were some strange bequests in the will."

"I'm surprised he didn't buy everyone a cup of coffee as well?" said Dudley Weston.

WPC Knowle stood up and moved into the middle of the room. "I was surprised to see such varying amounts given to each of you. The wording is a little unusual as well. Is there a reason for this?"

Dudley Musbury who had been silently sitting low in his chair raised his hand. "If I may hazard a guess?"

"Go on, Mr. Musbury."

"In my case, this sum of money is a surprisingly generous calculation of the money that Mr. Buckerell took off me as his fee."

The other Dudleys nodded.

"Blackmail money, more like, rather than a fee," grunted Dudley Weston.

"He's paid us back the money he stole off us all these years."

"Well, I must be off," said Doctor Moore, getting quickly to his feet. "I have some house calls to make. Mrs. Aylesbeare, please accept this verbal reply to my legacy. I shall not be taking one penny of that man's money. You may use my share however you wish! I'll put my reply in writing when I have time."

He gathered his coat and doctor's bag and made his way dramatically out of the room. In the silence, everyone could hear his footsteps rapidly descending the stairs to the street.

"Why didn't you go to the police if you were being blackmailed?" asked PC Hydon.

"I would have lost all my insurance money," griped Dudley Musbury. "In fact, with you two being here, I still may lose it."

"I'm afraid, Mr. Musbury," said PC Hydon, "we may need to reopen your case."

"Oh, great!" Dudley slumped even lower in his chair.

"We're all in trouble, it seems," added Dudley Gosford. "I always had my suspicions about his hold over me, but I couldn't afford to call his bluff. Now, it looks as if I have no alternative."

"Well, I'm in the clear. I paid him stupid sums of money so I could keep tabs on a woman. Not my wife, you understand. But now, I'm prepared to stand up and face any consequences."

"This is all well and good," said WPC Knowle, "but it gets us no nearer to solving Mr. Buckerell's death."

"Oh, I disagree," said Frank. "I think we're almost there."

Everyone turned to look at him. Frank moved into the centre of the room and peered around him. "What are you all doing next Monday?"

Dudley Gosford-Feniton stood up. His tall frame towered over Frank. "It's the dress rehearsal in the afternoon. Silly time to have it, I know. But we have to accommodate our star, the good doctor."

"Yes," said Dudley Weston. "We'll all be there."

"Good. I call a meeting after the dress rehearsal in the public hall at seven-thirty next Monday evening."

"Alice, Mrs. Aylesbeare, will you be able to attend?"

"I wouldn't miss it for the world!"

PC Hydon stood up. He was even taller than Dudley Gosford-Feniton. He gleefully rubbed his hands together.

"Eee, it's one of his Pierrots again," cried PC Hydon. "If you're the guilty one, you gotta be there. If 'ee don't attend, you'll be signalling your guilt to the rest of us. The innocent among you are perfectly safe!"

"Thank you, PC Hydon. No-one has to attend against their will. However, we look forward to your presence next Monday evening."

"Why?" asked Dudley Musbury.

"So," exclaimed Frank, "we can reveal Anthony Buckerell's

murderer."

CHAPTER 16
DEJA VU ONCE AGAIN

The next morning Frank and Elsie retrieved the whiteboard from the garage. Frank drew out the boxes and labelled them Suspect, Motive, Alibi, and Opportunity.

Ella recalled their previous attempts at drawing some semblance of logic out of the chaos. "First, let's list the suspects."

"The four Dudleys."

Frank wrote Dudley Gosford-Feniton, Dudley Weston, Dudley Musbury and Dudley Widworthy in the first four boxes on the left-hand side of the whiteboard.

In the fifth box, he wrote Alice Aylesbeare. Ella gasped. "You don't think..."

"Until we can eliminate her, we must include her in our thinking. Anybody else?"

"Mrs. Weston?" queried Ella.

"We can include her, but I can't see any connection between her and all of our investigations so far."

"Still, write her down. Just for completeness!"

Frank added her name in the sixth box.

"Motive," said Frank.

"Well, the four Dudleys were being blackmailed. Although we've eliminated her because of her name, Alice may have seen the will before she said she did."

"Yes, she may have seen her inheritance and her job for life," added Frank, "She could have passed on the information to one of the four Dudleys."

"And Mrs. Weston?" asked Ella.

"Well, she certainly loves her husband even if he doesn't love her."

"Unrequited love? Wouldn't she kill her husband in that situation? Sort of - if I can't have him, then no-one else will?"

"Good point!"

Ella stared at the whiteboard before clapping her hands in frustration. "No, no, wait a minute. We're missing something again!" said Ella.

"What?"

"Well, remember that phone call you received when we got back from our walk with Bella and George?"

"Yes, you're absolutely correct. Dudley's out to get me!"

"I'm happy to eliminate both Alice and Mrs. Weston!"

"Back to four Dudleys." Frank rubbed out the names of the two women.

"Well, in that case, do we need to write down Doctor Daniel Moore?"

"Yes!"

"But why?"

"Didn't you notice or was it just me? When Alice read out the will, Doctor Daniel Moore's middle names included Dudley. Sometimes people are called more often by their middle names than their first name."

"Another excellent point. How did I miss that?"

Frank tried to write Dr Daniel Aldous Huxley Dudley Moore

in the fifth box. "It's not going to fit!"

"Just call him Doctor Moore. For now!"

Frank did and stood back to look at the whiteboard. On to the next column?"

"No, we need to put in a motive for Doctor Moore?" Ella reminded him.

"Well, he wasn't being blackmailed."

"What about his three loves? The job, his plants and his drama. What about the licensing committee?"

"Could one of those be a reason to murder Anthony Buckerell? Hmm, maybe."

"The next column says Alibi."

"I noted down that every one of the Dudleys said that they had seen Anthony Buckerell in the days before he died."

Yes, so none of them has an alibi. They could have injected him with the poison without him even realising it. Then, with a little bit of calculation, send the note to him!"

"You went around to Anthony's office the day before he died. That was a Tuesday. That means that the poison was administered the day before that. Monday. In the evening at about eight o'clock."

"So, let's go back through our notes and see where our suspects were."

"Well, according to Daniel Moore, the four Dudleys all went to a meeting with Anthony Buckerell about the licensing."

"Strange that no one's mentioned a meeting with him before."

"If that was two days before the murder, then any one of them could have done it."

"We didn't ask the right questions, did we?"

"Where were you on Monday night?"

"And if none of the four Dudleys can provide us with an alibi then we have to assume they all had the opportunity."

"That phone caller said we weren't asking the right questions and we were stupid. They were right."

"No. We may not have been asking the right questions, but all the evidence is right in front of us. We're not stupid. They were wrong and we can prove it."

Frank and Ella added some vital information onto the whiteboard. They both turned towards each other. "We've done it!" They hugged and kissed as they celebrated the cutting down to size of another East Devon criminal.

Their elation didn't last too long as they realised that two questions needed answering that could bring an entirely different slant upon the investigation.

"Where were you on Monday night?"

"What was the meeting about?"

"Before we bring everybody together," said Frank, "I want to ask each of our suspects those two missing questions.

"Let's ask them separately and see if their answers agree."

"Let's ask Doctor Moore as well. See if he can shine any light on the matter."

They arranged to speak separately to each of them face to face during the course of the afternoon and evening. First, they went once again to Professor Gosford-Feniton's elegant house in the exclusive residential area north of the town.

"Monday night? Yes, we went to a meeting with Anthony Buckerell. About the licensing of this play."

"We?"

"The four Dudleys and two ladies. We were the elected negotiating committee. Daniel Moore was meant to be there, but he was on holiday."

Dudley Musbury and Dudley Widworthy were together when Frank and Ella asked the questions. Their answers were identical. Both of them were relieved to be able to tell the truth. Their accounts of the meeting were similar in tone to the Professor. They confirmed that the four Dudleys were in the group who met with Anthony Buckerell.

When Frank and Ella arrived at the Weston's house they were greeted by Mrs. Weston. "I'm afraid Dudley doesn't want to speak to you. He's sulking."

"Did he go out to a meeting on the Monday before Mr. Buckerell died?"

She thought for a moment. "Yes, he did. Something to do with the Budleigh Players, I think."

"Thank you, Mrs. Weston. That's all we needed to know."

Finally, later in the evening, after surgery had finished, they sat in Doctor Moore's consulting room and asked: "Where were you on the Monday before Mr. Buckerell died?"

"In London. About to board a plane to Thailand. I'm sure I've told your police officer friend that already."

"You're sure you weren't in Budleigh Salterton?"

"Positive. Why?"

"Because there was a meeting going on. It involved the Dramatic Society and Mr. Buckerell."

"Yes, I know. About the licensing. Glad I missed it. I'd have probably wanted to murder him if I was there."

"Good evening, Mr. Buckerell. Thank you for coming along to this informal gathering. Are any other members of your committee attending?"

"No, it's just me. I'll report back, of course, but the committee will go along with whatever I decide."

"I see. We'll come straight to the point, then. I'm Professor Dudley Gosford-Feniton. This is Mr. Weston, Mrs. Tidwell, Mr. Musbury, Miss Exton and Mr. Widworthy. We are all representing the Budleigh Players.

"Get on with it. I know who you all are. I've got another appointment in half an hour."

"OK. We are putting on the most ambitious play the Budleigh Players has ever produced."

"And we need a licence to perform it at the Public Halls. We have never had a problem obtaining this licence."

"Until now!"

"Yes, I'm well aware of your play. That's the problem."

"What's wrong with the play? There's no swearing, no gratuitous violence. It's family entertainment. It looks like we're going to be sold out on all three nights. The enquiries for tickets are at an all-time high."

"I don't care about any of that."

"What's the problem, then?"

"Your leading man."

"Daniel Moore?"

"Yes"

"This is his first leading role. He's perfect for the role."

"He may be. But if you want your dramatic production to take place, then you'd better have a word with him and persuade him to drop out. Find someone else to play his role."

"That's not possible."

"I could try. I'll give him a ring."

"Yes, you'd better. I refuse to grant a license if Daniel Moore is in the leading role."

"I'm beginning to get a feeling of deja-vu once again," said WPC Elsie Knowle, as she sat in the Raleigh's front room the next evening.

"Are you sure you know what you're doing?" asked PC Alf Hydon.

"Pretty sure. We've had the whiteboard out and filled in all the boxes."

"So, we're going to go all Murder in Paradise again?"

"Why not," replied Ella, "it worked last time."

"And I'll say what I said last time." Elsie looked slightly exasperated. "You can't just take over solving the crime. We're the police and it's our job to serve and protect you."

"Yes, but begging your pardon for my rudeness, but this time, you've spent hardly any time on the investigation. You keep telling us how busy you are."

"That's true!" Alf nodded.

"Point taken!" Elsie agreed.

"If we can get the murderer to confess then, once again, you'll get the credit."

"OK," said WPC Knowle, "I don't think my superiors need to know about this little scenario. I can see why you want to confront the murderer with the truth. If you can apply as much psychological pressure as possible, you'll have a confession made in front of everybody."

"Let's do it. Is there a door to guard?" asked Alf.

"No, we'll be in the middle of the auditorium at the Public Hall in Budleigh Salterton. It'll be difficult for anyone to quickly escape. Anyway, you'll be close at hand to apprehend them. The long arm of the law?"

PC Hydon stretched his right arm out in front of him. His open hand snapped shut.

"We'll sit them all down in the audience and you two can be

on stage."

"Just like a real play."

"No," said PC Hydon. "Imagine it, Stein and Cinders - mind readers extraordinaire - top of the bill."

WPC Knowle looked baffled. "Stein and Cinders?"

"Yes, Frank N Stein and Cinders Ella!"

"That's so preposterous that it might just work." Ella laughed.

Everyone laughed and made suggestions on how the two performers might construct their stage act.

Frank and Ella looked at each other. The two police officers were quickly joining in with the spirit of the occasion.

"Just remember," cautioned Ella, "we're attempting to catch a murderer."

Just like in Sidmouth, PC Hydon and WPC Knowle reminded the four Dudleys about the arrangements for the meeting after the dress rehearsal. They also invited Doctor Moore, Alice Aylesbeare and Mrs. Weston along.

WPC Knowle mused that the presence of three women amongst the group may lessen the chance of any violent or unruly behaviour. She had her own suspicions about the identity of the murderer but was willing to allow Frank and Ella to do things their way.

After all, if it was good enough for Hercule and a Caribbean copper, then it was good enough for her, too.

CHAPTER 17
THE DENOUEMENT

"Phone App working?"

"Yes!"

"Fully charged?"

"Of course! And now… switched on!"

"Ladies and Gentlemen, welcome to a special performance by Stein and Cinders."

The announcement by an unseen voice was broadcast over the loudspeaker system in the Public Hall. The Budleigh Player's rehearsal had finished a while ago. All those involved in the production had left the building except for the group sitting in the front row. The four Dudleys, Gosford-Feniton, Weston, Musbury and Widworthy, together with Doctor Daniel Moore, were sitting in the centre of the row looking uncertain and a little disorientated.

They had been there since the conclusion of the rehearsal talking quietly and awaiting developments. They were in a familiar place in an unfamiliar situation. They had been joined in the past few minutes by Mrs. Aylesbeare, Mrs. Weston, WPC Knowle and PC Hydon. The house lights had been kept dimmed since the rehearsal. As the curtain opened, the stage lights were illuminating not only the stage but the front two rows of the auditorium.

Ella came out from the wings and stood centre stage.

"Good evening and thanks to all of you for agreeing to attend our little meeting."

"Wouldn't have missed this for the world," cried out Dudley Weston. "Are you going to tell us who killed Anthony Buckerell?"

"We're going to present some facts and allow you to draw your conclusions."

"First of all, let me introduce you all to each other. My name is Ella Raleigh. I'm joined by my husband, Frank."

Frank ventured on stage holding a clipboard.

"It's Dennis Norden!" shouted Dudley Weston.

"That'll do, Weston. Give them a chance." Dudley Gosford-Feniton's voice was quiet but firm.

"We have in the front row the four Dudleys, Gosford-Feniton, Weston, Musbury and Widworthy, accompanied by Doctor Daniel Moore. Behind them, in the second row, we have Mrs. Alice Aylesbeare, Mrs. Weston and WPC Knowle. Over by the fire doors, we have PC Hydon."

"Get on with it. Some of us have got lives to lead," muttered Daniel Moore.

Ella continued. "As you know, Anthony Buckerell died in the police cell at Otterbury Police Station."

"Both WPC Knowle and I were with him and our first thoughts were that he had died of a heart attack. In a way, we were correct." Frank stepped back.

"In fact, Mr. Buckerell died as a result of poisoning. He had been injected with Thamacin. It is a deadly poison extracted from a plant found only in South East Asia. A small amount of this poison causes a fatal heart attack exactly two days after the administering of the poison. The poison clogs up the arteries around the heart and after exactly forty-eight hours, the heart ceases to function."

Frank continued. "I'm sure you've worked out that Anthony Buckerell may well have died in the cell, but the poisonous injection was administered two days previously."

Mrs. Aylesbeare let out a gasp of surprise.

"So," asked Ella, "who murdered Anthony Buckerell?"

"To begin with, we need to consider the three factors behind most premeditated murders."

"Motive," announced Ella.

"Opportunity."

"And means."

The Frank and Ella show continued.

"We looked at each of the Dudleys…"

"Why just us," piped up Dudley Musbury.

"Because," continued Ella, "we received a phone call from Anthony Buckerell entirely by chance."

"Our phone number is exactly the same as WPC Knowle's private number, except that the last two digits are reversed."

"Anthony was in such a state that he almost dialled the number he was intending to ring."

"His cry for help stated that Dudley was out to get him," Frank added.

"After some research, it transpires that four Dudleys, all clients of his, sent him letters of complaint. All four Dudleys, it turns out, were being blackmailed by Anthony Buckerell."

"We looked at each of the Dudleys and deduced, that all four of you had a motive to harm Anthony Buckerell."

"Each of you considered the blackmail to be both unfair and life-changing."

"We interviewed each of you and you all showed a degree of animosity towards the deceased."

"Having confirmed a motive, we then went on to opportunity," Ella concluded the motives.

"Wait a minute. I agree with your comments so far, in respect of my motive. I told him, I wanted to kill him," said Dudley Widworthy.

"Yes, then we went to the reading of the will," added Dudley Weston. "Each of us got our blackmail money back. In fact, I for one am better off than I was!"

"However, none of you knew the contents of the will at the time of the murder," replied Ella.

"True. But why are these other people here?" Dudley Widworthy pointed behind him and then towards Doctor Moore.

Frank took up the explanation. "WPC Knowle and PC Hydon are here to make sure that law and order and justice prevails. Mrs. Aylesbeare is here because she has helped us throughout the course of our enquiries and, it's only right and proper, that she hears the full story of how her employer died."

"Is she a suspect?" shouted Dudley Weston.

"We've already ruled her out. Mrs. Weston demanded to be here."

"So that Doreen can keep an eye on me."

"If you say so, Mr. Weston."

"And Doctor Moore is here because he is," Ella paused for effect. "The fifth Dudley!"

"You've got that wrong. My name is Daniel, not Dudley. I thought I was here because of my medical expertise."

"You are. But," Frank replied, "although your first name is Daniel, one of your middle names is Dudley. I believe that Anthony Buckerell was extremely fond of the jazz piano."

Mrs. Aylesbeare nodded in agreement.

"He nicknamed you Dudley Moore."

"Who was, as you know, not only a comedian but also a talented jazz pianist."

"When we realised that possibility then we looked around for a motive. This drama production provided us with a motive. You were all set to achieve your life's ambition - a starring role."

"Mr. Anthony Buckerell's committee were going to prevent your starring role by refusing the Budleigh Players a licence for their production."

"Rubbish. They granted our licence. We've been rehearsing this evening, haven't we?" Daniel Moore aggressively countered.

"Let's come back to that in a while. Opportunity," said Frank.

"Every Dudley here had the opportunity to poison Anthony. Four of you met up with him in the days before his death. You could easily have manufactured a further meeting and then injected him."

"Doctor Moore. You used to regularly inject Mr. Buckerell with his vitamins."

"Yes, but that was days before his death. You said Thamacin takes effect in exactly forty-eight hours."

"I'll give you an answer to that comment in a few minutes. First of all, Ella wants to explore the exotic plants you collect."

"Yes, we've concluded that each of you had the motive and the opportunity to murder Anthony Buckerell. Now, what about the means?"

Mrs. Aylesbeare's face was a picture of subdued excitement. She was imagining herself as a witness in an episode of Miss Marple.

"Professor Gosford-Feniton, you're an expert in African plants?"

"Correct."

"Just African and not Asian?"

"Correct. You are welcome to check my records at any time."

"Thank you. We believe you, but we will - if we need to. Now, Dudley Weston. Your specialism is ferns from New Zealand?"

"Yes, you know that already. You've been to see them all. Nothing from Asia. Again, check my records."

Doreen Weston nodded in approval.

"Mr. Widworthy?"

"All my herbs were from South America. That was a long time ago. You can check my records as well. And, I'm sure, Mrs. Aylesbeare will be able to find Anthony Buckerell's records from our transactions!"

"Mr. Musbury?"

"I've never collected exotic plants or made poisons from them. I spent all my waking time looking after my wife. Please feel free to search my old house."

"So none of you, travelled to Asia or dealt with Asian plants?"

"Except one. Daniel Aldous Huxley Dudley Moore."

All eyes turned towards the doctor.

"You regularly visit Thailand. The poison came from a plant called," Ella consulted Frank's clipboard. "Ot-tan Etti-na-reem. Our research found out that a Jesuit priest called Father Amuccin discovered it whilst travelling in Siam in South East Asia. Siam, as you know, nowadays goes under the name of Thailand."

"You regularly visit Thailand? Your receptionist told us you go every year. As regular as clockwork!"

"But I wasn't in Budleigh Salterton when you say the poison was administered!"

"No, you say you were in the process of travelling to Thailand."

"Or were you?" ventured WPC Knowle. "According to my investigations, the airline has no record of you travelling to

Thailand three days before Mr. Buckerell's death."

"That's rubbish. They must have made a mistake."

"Maybe, but they do have a record of a Daniel Moore travelling the day before Mr. Buckerell's death. It's a common name. Could that be you? Or is it just coincidence?"

Dudley Musbury raised a hand. "Excuse me."

"Yes, Dudley," said Ella.

"As Stage Manager and not an actor or writer, I was the one nominated to phone Dudley about our meeting. I didn't think anything of it until this evening."

"What did you tell him?"

"That he had to give up the starring role or else Anthony Buckerell would get the committee to refuse the licence."

"When did you call him?"

"I've just been working it out. It must have been about three days before Mr. Buckerell died. I called him on his mobile. It sounded like he was in a railway station or an... airport." Dudley Musbury looked as if a lightbulb had just been switched on inside his head. "He was at Heathrow!"

WPC Knowle stood up and turned towards the doctor. "So you travelled back to Budleigh Salterton and gave Anthony Buckerell one more injection?"

"Except this time, it wasn't vitamins but Thamacin," concluded Ella.

Daniel Moore looked like a rabbit caught in the headlights of a ten-ton lorry.

"I'm a star. He couldn't take that away from me. He may be able to bamboozle your lives with his blackmailing ways but not me. I'm better than you people- I'm a star."

CHAPTER 18
A STAR IN THE HEAVENS

"Daniel Moore, you are under arrest for the murder of Anthony Buckerell!" WPC Knowle stood up and manoeuvred herself out of the second row.

"I think not," shouted Doctor Moore.

He pushed past the statuesque Dudleys and made his way towards the main exit at the rear of the auditorium. PC Hydon stood in his way.

"Not so fast, sir. You're going nowhere. Stand exactly where you are!"

Doctor Moore ignored his command. He double-backed towards the stage. The four Dudleys scattered to all the points of the compass. Doreen Weston screamed. Mrs. Aylesbeare had taken her phone out and was filming every second of the action with a delighted smile on her face.

Doctor Moore clambered up the side steps and tried to push despairingly past Frank.

Frank did not budge so he moved towards centre stage before heading towards the rear of the stage. The scenery flaps were in his way.

WPC Knowle and Frank advanced towards him. He grabbed hold of Ella from behind. "Move away! If you get too close, I'll hurt her, really hurt her."

Frank stopped frozen to the spot. WPC Knowle paused her advance and shouted to PC Hydon. "Alf, call for back-up. Now!!!"

Doctor Moore shuffled backwards again towards the scenery flaps. He pushed with his foot looking for a gap and a possible getaway. As he did so, Ella forced all her weight down-wards and stabbed both her feet on Doctor Moore's trailing foot. Instinctively he let go so he could hit out at her. Ella beat him to it. She kicked him in the one place she was certain he would not appreciate being kicked in. Doctor Moore screamed out an Anglo-Saxon sounding word and tumbled backwards into the scene flap.

Ella rolled away from his grasp. Doctor Moore hit the floor but quickly stood back up. Then his feet began rising in the air and within a couple of seconds, his whole body had turned upside down. He continued rising in the air until he was suspended upside down about seven foot above the stage.

"What the... Get me down!"

One of the ropes used to pull the scene flaps up and out of the audience's sight had become wrapped around his legs. The more he struggled, the worse he became entangled. Everyone heard a creaking noise and Dudley Musbury appeared on stage.

"That should keep him there until reinforcements arrive."

Ella burst out laughing. "Thank heavens for an untidy stage manager!"

Doctor Moore still struggled but it only made matters worse.

"Get me down."

Everyone just stood on stage and watched.

"The blood's rushing to my head."

Mrs. Aylesbeare continued videoing on her phone.

"I could get brain damage!"

"Bit late for that," said Dudley Musbury.

Doctor Moore shook his body in an effort to break free. A clear plastic bag slipped from his pocket and landed on the stage.

"Hello," said PC Hydon, "What do we have here?" He picked up the bag and immediately recognised a syringe and a small test-tube full of a murky brown liquid.

"Be careful, Alf," said Frank. "I think that may be our conclusive evidence."

"Why don't we inject the good doctor with it and see what happens in forty-eight hours' time?" shouted Dudley Weston.

"No. Don't touch it," screamed Doctor Moore, "you can't kill a star."

"A star?" chortled Dudley Widworthy. "Well, I suppose, at this precise moment, you're nearer to the heavens than we are!"

"Yes, just one more star in the heavens!"

"Except this one's about to flicker and fade away."

CHAPTER 19
COFFEE AT EARLS

Police reinforcements arrived swiftly from Exeter. They included the Assistant Chief Constable. The fire brigade and ambulance both attended the scene. They carefully released Doctor Moore from his rope entanglement and checked him over for any injuries. They found no more damage other than wounded pride. He was soon whisked away in a flurry of police cars to Exeter police station.

"Well done, everybody. I thought my idea of community assistance would produce results."

Frank and Ella looked at each other and smiled.

WPC Knowle and PC Hydon nodded and bit their tongues.

The next day the four Dudleys of Budleigh along with Doreen, Alice, Ella and Frank spent some considerable time providing statements to the police. Alice's video was transferred from her phone to a police tape. Ella surrendered her audio recording and both WPC Knowle and PC Hydon reassured them all that the evidence was certain to convict Doctor Daniel

Moore of murder.

A week later the eight of them sat together discussing the events of the past few weeks whilst drinking coffee at Earls.

"Did any of you suspect Daniel Moore of murdering Anthony Buckerell?"

The four Dudleys all shook their heads.

"I thought it was one of you three," said the Professor looking around at the three other Dudleys.

"I was sure it was you, Frank," said Dudley Weston. "I couldn't understand how else he could have been killed." He coughed and looked Frank straight in the eyes. "I'd like to apologise with all my heart for the anguish I caused you. Looking back now, it was unforgivable. I'd also like to thank you for your kind, supportive words to Totnes police. Because of you, they've dropped the charges. I've been let off with a warning not to do it again. I've given them my word I won't!"

"I will make sure he keeps his word," said Doreen.

"That cottage was a dump!" moaned Ella.

"Not anymore," replied Doreen. "We're doing it up. It's our little project for the next year or so. It's going to be our little bolt hole."

"Or our love nest," smiled Dudley Weston.

Ella thought the look on Doreen's face was priceless.

There was a moment of quietness punctuated by the clink of china cups and the slurping of hot coffee.

"We'd been receiving some mysterious telephone calls whilst we were investigating Anthony's death," said Ella.

"It was only during the trouble at the Public Hall that I realised who it was," added Frank.

"Daniel Moore?"

"Yes, during our conversations with him he used the word bamboozled. I've only ever heard the word bamboozle a couple of times since we've been in Devon. And each time I heard it from him. He used it again at the Public Hall."

Frank nodded.

"He may have been a good doctor, but he was not a nice man," said Dudley Widworthy, "Not once in my time with Mr. Buckerell did I really think of killing him. I may have said it, I may have thought it, but I would never have carried it out. You just don't do things like that."

"Daniel did."

"Yes, and look where it got him."

There was more clinking and slurping.

"Another cup, anyone?" said Alice.

More hot coffee was dispensed, and Alice changed the subject. "How's your wife, Mr. Musbury?"

"She's making some good progress. She's finally responding to the treatment they've been giving her. They're thinking of a hip replacement. She may even be able to walk again one day." There was light and life in Daniel Musbury's eyes. Ella had never seen him like this before.

"What about you, Alice? Any luck on the job front?" asked Ella.

"I put some adverts in some of the law journals. I've had some enquiries from potentially interested parties. That's all I'm prepared to say at present!"

The conversation drifted on to lighter matters. There was even some laughter. There was a sense of relief that the whole ordeal was over, and life could be looked forward to once again.

"Now here's a funny thing," said Dudley Widworthy. "Now that Daniel's unable to take the starring role in our forthcoming production, you'll be pleased to know that we asked Dudley Musbury to take an acting part. He's agreed to take on Dudley Weston's role."

"What about Dudley Weston?" asked Ella.

"Oh, don't worry about him. He's been offered Daniel's star role. My Dudley's going to be a star!" cried Doreen.

Ella clapped her hands in delight.

"Did I ever tell you about the time I was collecting plants in Tanzania when a herd of elephants came wandering my way?"

"Yes!" chorused the other three Dudleys. "Many times!"

There was laughter, heartfelt laughter whilst Dudley Gosford-Feniton looked momentarily confused. Then he shrugged his shoulders and joining in with the good-humoured atmosphere.

Later, as they were preparing to leave the establishment, all four Dudleys raised a hand and asked for quiet.

Dudley Weston was their spokesman. "On behalf of the Dudleys of Budleigh, I'd like to thank all of you, but especially Frank and Ella, for their hard work in solving our little problem. As a token of our appreciation, we'd like to invite you to join us at the Public Hall for next week's opening night of the Budleigh Player's production of Table for Four written and directed by Dudley Gosford-Feniton."

"Delighted!" cried Ella.

A week later at a packed Public Hall, a good time was had by all.

POSTSCRIPT

If you want to help spread the word about the book, then I'd appreciate it if you left a review on my Amazon book page. Please do it now!

If you want to receive up to date information about the East Devon Cosy Mysteries, please sign up for our newsletter. Newsletter subscribers will receive 6 walks in and around Sidmouth, an eBook that includes the walks Ella and Frank enjoyed in both *The Dudleys of Budleigh* and *Cidered in Sidmouth.*

To subscribe and to find out more about Frank and Ella Raleigh and their East Devon Cosy Mysteries please visit East Devon Cosy Mysteries, the author's website.

The author, PA Nash can be reached on:

Facebook

www.facebook.com/pa.nash.182

Twitter

twitter.com/PANash49873070

Pinterest

www.pinterest.co.uk/EastDevonCosyMysteries/

or by

Email

info@eastdevoncosymysteries.com

A GOOD WALK

Solvitur Ambulando

A Latin phrase meaning "it is solved by walking." A good walk brings a new perspective on your problems and often allows you to solve them.

WEST DOWN BEACON

Difficulty - Moderate - Paths, tracks and quiet roads, some ascent and descent

Start - Budleigh Salterton Public Hall - EX9 6RW

Finish - Budleigh Salterton Public Hall

Length - 3.8 miles (6.0 km)

Summary - Inland, this walk travels along the route of the old railway line, through scenic woodland which is home to an abundance of wildlife, including bats and lizards. Along the coast, there are stunning red cliffs, and the remains of a signal station built to warn of enemy vessels during the Napoleonic Wars.

Public Transport - Buses run regularly between Exmouth and Sidmouth, stopping at Knowle Corner and Little Knowle. For timetable information visit Traveline or phone 0871 200 22 33.

Nearest car park - At the Public Hall in Station Road, Budleigh Salterton. Postcode EX9 6RJ

Nearest toilets – Behind the Public Hall.

Nearest refreshments – In Budleigh Salterton, or the Dog and Donkey in Knowle

ROUTE DESCRIPTION

1. From Budleigh Salterton's Public Hall walk northwards up Station Road, carrying on along Moor Lane to come out at the top of Dark Lane, by the school.

2. Turn right onto Dark Lane, and then almost immediately left, to carry on in the original direction up Bedlands Lane.

3. From the top of Bedlands Lane turn left onto the B3178 and then right a moment later, to walk up Bear Lane.

4. At the railway bridge pick up the cycle path on your left, leading towards Exmouth, and follow it through the woods to Castle Lane.

This is part of the Budleigh-Exmouth Cycleway, which here runs along the former railway line which linked Budleigh Salterton and Exmouth.

Work started on the railway line in 1899, and it took four years for the labourers to construct its numerous bridges and embankments and cut its path through Knowle Hill. They did this using picks and shovels, with the help of two 'steam navvies' - steam shovels - which they employed at either end of the cutting, to meet in the middle. The line never reached its full potential, however, and by the 1950s was scarcely used at all. In 1963 it fell foul of the infamous Beeching report, '*The Reshaping of British Railways*' and the last train ran in 1967.

As is the case elsewhere, however, the rail traveller's loss is the walker's and cyclist's gain. Many of the former railway lines in the south-west have been redeployed as cycle paths and footpaths. Most of these are broad and flat and have been surfaced with tarmac, making the peaceful countryside they travel through, accessible to a wide range of users.

In a tidy piece of history, the Budleigh-Exmouth Cycleway

was officially opened in 1998 by Lord Clinton, a relative of Mrs. Williams-Drummond, daughter of Lady Gertrude Rolle and the honorary driver of the first train from Tipton St John to Budleigh, in 1897.

The surrounding woods and hedges are home to a plethora of wildlife, including foxes and badgers, dormice and bats, adders and lizards, and butterflies, dragonflies and rare wood crickets.

5. Turn left up onto the path to Castle Lane, turning onto the lane at the top to head roughly southwards.

6. When Castle Lane turns sharply right, take the footpath ahead which continues in your direction, and follow this alongside the Golf Club for about a mile, ignoring the Littleham Church path which crosses yours, also ignoring the detours to the left shortly afterwards. Follow the waymarkers around to the right when they cross the golf course, turning off again to the left at the end.

Be aware of the golfers around you and the possibility of flying balls as you cross the golf course and keep dogs under control here.

7. Turn left when you come to the South West Coast Path and follow it for about three–quarters of a mile towards Budleigh Salterton.

East Devon is particularly noteworthy for its red sandstone formations, dating back to the Triassic period, some 245- 240 million years ago. The red cliffs here are a sample of the stunning rock formations which have earned the 'Jurassic Coast' of East Devon and Dorset World Heritage status.

At the highest point on this part of the coast, you will come to a trig point. This is West Down Beacon, once a fire beacon, and later a signal station during the Napoleonic Wars.

By 1795, before the Napoleonic Wars began, Britain was already in conflict with France and the Admiralty needed a faster means of communication than the current system of horseback messengers. A network of signal stations was established, connecting the Admiralty in London with its fleet ports along the south coast. These included Dawlish Head and Berry Head on one side of West Down Beacon, and Peak Hill and Beer Head on the other.

This was before the invention of the electrical telegraph, and the signalling system used was known as an optical telegraph, which required a direct line of sight between the signal stations. Standing on West Down Beacon on a good day, you can see why it was chosen: there is excellent visibility in all directions.

Signals consisted of flags and balls, and the system warned merchant vessels as well as RN cruisers of where the French privateers were lurking. Signals used included: 1 ball above a flag for an enemy frigate or frigates; 2 balls above a flag for a small cruiser; 3 balls above a flag for an enemy vessel close under the land. Eventually, this system was replaced with a semaphore telegraph - a high pole with hinged signal arms, ironically devised by the French themselves during the Napoleonic Wars!

The signal stations were also used to warn of suspected smuggling activities, and if goods were seized as a result of information received in this way, the signal station concerned would be entitled to a share of the booty.

8. From West Down Beacon the Coast Path descends gently into Budleigh Salterton. Carry on along it, past the first few houses, until you come to an open green area. At the far end of this field turn left, to walk up Victoria Place and onto the B3178 road beyond.

9. Turn right here, and then take the next left, into Station Road, to return to the start of the walk.

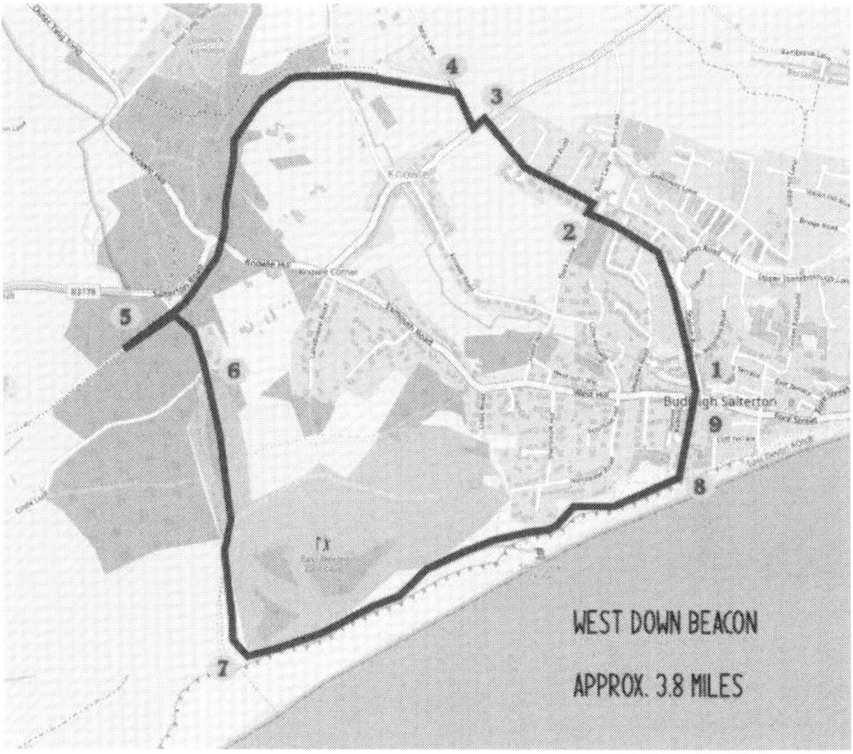
WEST DOWN BEACON
APPROX. 3.8 MILES
Budleigh Salterton
1
2
3
4
5
6
7
8
9

ABOUT THE AUTHOR

PA Nash and his supportive wife moved to glorious East Devon nearly a decade ago having taken early retirement from his previous job in South East England. Not quite ready for a life of endless relaxation, PA has since dabbled as a website administrator for the South West Coast Path, an IT office assistant in a local school and a WordPress website designer. This is his second cosy mystery book. The others in the series are also available on the Kindle and in paperback from Amazon.

I've read so many cosy mystery novels in the past ten years. Some series like MC Beaton's Hamish Macbeth and Agatha Raisin were excellent, others not so!

I thought I could put together a series based around an area of England. Everyone's written about the Cotswolds and the Midsomer counties, so I thought it would be best to avoid those areas. We live in a beautiful part of the South West of England. East Devon is full of quaint villages, relaxing towns, peaceful countryside and hidden gems. It's just waiting for a few juicy murders! The police presence is minimal. The population is not as full of old-aged pensioners as some would have you believe. Perhaps it's time to create a rival to Midsomer!

I enjoy walking so I've made use of the South West Coast Path and other footpaths in my books. Each book will have a selection of walks most reasonably fit people can complete. Some of the walks can be found on the excellent South West Coast Path Association's website.

I intend to create a series of short cosy mysteries based around the towns and villages of East Devon.

ALSO AVAILABLE

"This is Sidmouth, sir. Nobody gets murdered in Sidmouth!"

Newly retired Frank and Ella Raleigh didn't expect to be confronted with an upturned body in a cider barrel. WPC Knowle called it a tragic accident, Frank and Ella didn't agree. Guess who was right?

The **first** book in the East Devon Cosy Mysteries series, **Cidered in Sidmouth**, introduces coastal walks, cider farms, cliff-top drama and a traditional Golden Age denouement as Frank and Ella solve a very unusual murder in this quiet old-fashioned seaside town.

I'm giving away Kennaway Coopers, my company, to the winner of the Ottery Lottery!"

Caleb Kennaway's family and the other board members violently disagreed with his decision. A month later, Caleb Kennaway was found dead at the foot of the main stairs in Kennaway Court.

The third book in the East Devon Cosy Mystery series finds Frank and Ella Raleigh buying a ticket in the Ottery Lottery.

This leads them into an opportunity to investigate Caleb's death as well as a hunt for a miniature beer barrel that will change their lives.

Pop backstage into the world of 60's chart star Cornelius Spooner for a mixture of music, murder and cosy mystery.

Meet Cornelius, his band, the Portobello Crooners and his six wives.

During a quiet weekend away at a Country House Hotel near Lyme Regis, Frank and Ella Raleigh find themselves caught up in their deadliest case yet.

Accidents? Murders? Suspects with alibis, motives and opportunities - it's all there.

The following is a brief sample from the opening chapters of **The Ottery Lottery**.

CHAPTER ONE

Since all that beat about in Nature's range,
Or veer or vanish; why should'st thou remain
The only constant in a world of change

"Sometimes you make me want to kill you!" Christine screamed.

"The feeling's mutual." Caleb turned towards her, almost spitting out the words.

"Why? After all the hard work. Why?"

"Because it's my money and I want to have some fun with it."

"What about me?"

"You're well provided for. You always have been and you always will be."

"I don't understand you. I'm not sure I ever will!"

"Perhaps that's the problem."

Christine changed tack. "Doesn't Kenneth mean anything to you?"

"Yes, it's about time he stood on his own two feet."

"And Fabian and Carl? Have you told them? Don't they have a say?"

"Why do you think I asked them both to come here this evening? They're only directors. They can't outvote me. They'll do what I say. They always do."

A moment of silence descended upon the room as if they were preparing for the next onslaught. The calm before the storm.

There was a knock at the front door and Caleb went to open it.

"Come in, Fabian. Is Carl not with you?"

"No. Am I late?"

"You're never late. Come into the drawing-room and I'll pour you a drink."

Fabian followed Caleb into the room and sat down in one of the comfortable armchairs by the piano.

"Good evening, Fabian." A curt sharp voice greeted the man.

"Good evening, Mrs. Kennaway." He would never dare to call her Christine.

Caleb brought Fabian his drink and handed another to Christine. She looked at him and for a moment, Caleb thought she might throw it back into his face.

"Where's Kenneth?"

"I'll call him," muttered Christine. She pulled out her mobile phone from her trouser pocket and dialled a number. "Kenneth, come down. We're almost ready to start."

Within half a minute they could hear the echo of footsteps on the stone stairs leading down into the front hall. There was another knock at the front door.

"I'll get it," a voice from the hall shouted.

"Good evening, Carl. We're in the drawing-room. Come

through!"

Kenneth ushered the well-built man into the room. He was puffing and appeared out of breath. "Sorry, meeting finished a bit late."

"Sit down, Carl. Drink?"

"Yes, please."

After drinks had been dispensed and sipped, everyone sat down. Over the past few years, they each seemed to possess their allotted chair and drink. They all sat and drank as if in a trance. Caleb was the last to be seated. The rest of the room turned their eyes towards him. He had their undivided attention.

"I've brought you together this evening because I thought you deserved to hear the news, straight from the horse's mouth, as it were."

He smiled but no-one smiled back.

"I've decided to give up the chair and ownership of Kennaway Coopers. I'm retiring. I have enough money saved to keep on enjoying my lovely lifestyle, so I've...." He stopped to savour the moment.

"Oh, Caleb, stop messing around and tell them." Christine's voice stabbed into the expectant atmosphere.

"Alright, my dear." Caleb had a twinkle in his eyes and a smile upon his lips.

"I've already communicated this information with my wife. If you were anywhere in Ottery St Mary, you will have heard her reaction!"

He took a sip of his drink.

"Get on with it!" his wife snapped.

"I'm retiring and none of you will be taking my place as Chair or owner."

There was a sharp intake of breath from the gathered group.

"What do you mean?" blustered Kenneth.

"What I mean is that the company I've built from nothing, Kennaway Coopers–well, I will be giving it away."

There was an explosion of noise in the room.

Caleb held up his hand and shouted above the tumult. "I'm giving it away to the winner of the Ottery Lottery!"

"Ladies and Gentlemen, members of the press. Welcome to Kennaway Court. I've invited you here this morning to announce the Ottery Lottery."

Four journalists stood in the drawing-room of Kennaway Court with notebooks and dictaphones in hand as Caleb Kennaway spoke.

"Over one year ago, I decided it was time to retire. Kennaway Coopers, makers of the famous Tar Barrels of Ottery is a thriving, dependable business. Under my tutelage, the company has a well-deserved reputation for reliable delivery, quality products and outstanding customer service. When I looked around at my potential successors, I could not honestly say that any of them could be trusted to continue to run the company to the same high standards."

The lady from the Ottery Gazette held up her hand. The other three were furiously scribbling. "Does you mean that Kennaway Coopers is closing down?"

"No, far from it. I hope it will continue to produce quality tar barrels for many years to come. I have a dedicated, skilled workforce. I have no wish to see them made redundant or out of work."

"Good," said the Gazette lady, "My husband has spent twenty years of his life working for you."

"I know, Rosemary, and I genuinely hope he has a job with the company for at least another twenty years. However, although the workforce may be first class, the same cannot be said for the rest of the management team!"

"Oh, Mr. Kennaway, that's not very nice. Do you really want us to print that?"

"If you want to, I don't really care."

Caleb paused for breath.

"What I do care about is the Ottery Lottery. Let me explain. I will be selling tickets for the Ottery Lottery from this day onwards for one month only. During the next thirty days, anyone can buy a ticket. They are reasonably priced at £25 each. In one month's time, there will be a grand draw here at Kennaway Court and the winner of the Ottery Lottery will be the new owner and chair of Kennaway Coopers. The only stipulation I am going to make is that I would want the name of the company to remain the same."

The man from the Echo put down his pen and raised a hand. "So you're going to give the company away? For free?"

"Well, each ticket will cost £25. There will be no limits on how many tickets each person can buy."

"I assume you'll pocket the proceeds?"

"No. It's all going to go to a charity run by my wife. A charity that builds communes for orphaned children in Albania. It's called People's Orphanage Commune Albania. We call it POCA. But it's no gamble on our part. My wife receives no salary from the charity. Neither do I. Every pound raised will go to POCA. No top-slicing. No backhanders. All fair and above board."

"Talking of fair and above board. How can my readers be assured that this Lottery will be fair?"

"I have appointed a firm of solicitors from Budleigh Salterton to oversee the proceedings. I have given them full access to every meeting and every transaction."

A familiar figure walked into the room.

"May I introduce Alice Aylesbeare to you. She is the administrator at Buckerells of Budleigh. She may appear sweet and grandmotherly, but don't try to cross her. Her bite is much worse than her bark!"

Alice and Caleb fielded a few more questions before Caleb wrapped up the meeting.

"Thank you, everyone, for attending. Please publicise the Ottery Lottery far and wide. I look forward to meeting up with you again in one month's time."

Frank and Ella Raleigh stood outside the white walls of Exeter Crown and County Court with a look of relief on both their faces. They had just emerged through the revolving door having completed their stint as witnesses in a murder trial. The local paper had labelled the case as the Dudleys of Budleigh and both Frank and Ella had played an important role in bringing the murderer to justice.

For now, they were desperate to travel back to their home in the sleepy town of Otterbury and continue their lives as retired schoolteachers. In the past six months, they had become investigators in two cases of murder, they had been threatened, kidnapped and, on one occasion, Ella had been almost killed. Enough was enough. They agreed that it was time to go back to the quiet life.

As they were preparing to walk to their car, they heard a cry of "Oo-ee, Frank. Ella!" They turned around to see where it had come from and emerging from the revolving doors appeared Mrs. Aylesbeare, the solicitor's secretary from Budleigh Salterton. Frank and Ella waited as a small well-rounded lady caught up with them. Ella was reminded of the first time they had met her. She was still wearing her ankle-length patterned woollen coat and a flowery hat-this time the hat was green in colour. As usual, she carried her large brown corduroy handbag. She still reminded Frank of Miss Marple-straight from the pages of one of Agatha Christie's novels.

"Alice," called Ella, "have you finished as well?"

"Yes, but so has the trial. It took the jury so little time to come to their verdict."

"What was the verdict?"

"Guilty, of course. What else could it be?"

"Can we offer you a lift back to Budleigh?"

"No, it's OK. I've got my own car now. It's a 1979 Triumph Spitfire. Red, of course!"

"I didn't even know you could drive."

"Oh yes, ever since I was a young girl. I bought the car with my inheritance."

"Yes, of course. It's like you've won the lottery!"

All three of them began walking back to the car park on the other side of Magdalen Street.

"Speaking of the lottery," Alice said, "have you bought your ticket for the Ottery Lottery yet?"

"The what...?"

"The Ottery Lottery. I'd have thought you would have known all about it. It's in your part of the valley. You must have read it in the local paper?"

"No," said Ella, "we've been rather pre-occupied recently."

"Well, Caleb Kennaway who owns Kennaway Coopers is selling his company. They make the barrels that all the pubs in Ottery use on Tar Barrel Night. Why don't you pop into Ottery and get your ticket? You never know, you could be Kennaway Coopers next owner!"

They reached the carpark and both Frank and Ella nodded in admiration as Alice jumped into her Triumph Spitfire, revved up the engine and waved them farewell. The sound of the fiery red Triumph could be heard above the rest of the busy traffic as it made its way along Magdalen Street and off down the Topsham Road back to Budleigh.

Later that week, Frank and Ella drove into Ottery St Mary. With its parish church on the hill and its independent shops spreading out from the town square, the place had history. It had appeared in the Domesday Book. Its school, King's was a former grammar school founded by Henry the Eighth in 1545. The River Otter passed through the western edge of the town. Samuel Taylor Coleridge, he of the Ancient Mariner poem, was born in the town. It had Tar Barrel Night in November and Pixie Day in June. In 1866 the Great Fire of Ottery destroyed about a quarter of the town. In 1980 a commercial plane crashed landed in a nearby field narrowly avoiding the town. The only casualties were two sheep.

Ottery was not your bland, could-be-anywhere town.

Frank and Ella parked in the Canaan Way car park and made their way past the supermarket toward The Square. Ella stopped a middle-aged man loitering outside a hardware shop. "Excuse me, where do I buy my Ottery Lottery ticket?"

"Over there." He pointed at a trestle table set up on the road outside the council offices.

Sitting behind the table were two burly gentlemen, one dressed in a bright red cardigan and the other wearing a blue baseball cap with the words Kennaway Coopers emblazoned on it. They both stood up as Ella approached. "Good morning, how may we help you?" said the red cardiganed one.

"I'd like to buy a ticket for the Ottery Lottery."

"Not a problem. Each ticket costs twenty-five pounds. You can buy as many as you want."

"Thank you. Just one, please."

The baseball cap joined in. "You'll need to fill in this form.

We'll need your name and a contact number. Just in case, you win."

The red cardigan continued the double act. "Also, please read the rules carefully. Every penny you spend on a ticket will be going to support the Commune Charity in Albania.

Baseball cap's turn. "There's a leaflet at the other end of the table describing all about the charity. Please take one if you wish."

Ella read and then filled in the form. She handed over her money which was promptly put away in a blue steel money box with the Kennaway logo stencilled across the lid.

"Do you both work for Mr. Kennaway?" asked Ella.

"Yes, ma'am. We both left school on the Friday and started work at the Coopers on the next Monday. Didn't get a summer holiday that year." The blue baseball cap sounded proud and loyal.

"We're the senior workers, so we've been entrusted the task of selling these tickets. Also, we can check out our potential future boss."

"The only way you can buy a ticket is through us."

"You sound very organised. I'm most impressed."

"Thank you, ma'am." A small queue had built up behind Frank and Ella.

"Excuse us, ma'am, here's your ticket. Good luck."

Frank and Ella moved away and, seeing it was just after eleven o'clock, found themselves a local coffee shop in which they were happy to while away some time.

Over in Kennaway Court, four people were discussing the events of the past week.

"I've been to see a solicitor In Exeter. He's allowed to do this.

He can't be challenged."

"I'll challenge him. I'll put my hands around his throat and throttle him."

"That'll do no good. I bet he's changed his will."

"He's enjoying himself. I've never seen him look so happy and relaxed."

"I'm so angry with him."

"We all are!"

"We're sitting here talking. Isn't anyone going to take any action?"

"What sort of action."

"Extreme, drastic action."

Printed in Great Britain
by Amazon

62963801R00116